ONE YEAR IN AFRICA

1964–65

HANS VAN DEN HOUTEN

authorHOUSE®

AuthorHouse™
1663 Liberty Drive
Bloomington, IN 47403
www.authorhouse.com
Phone: 1 (800) 839-8640

Published by AuthorHouse   12/14/2016

ISBN: 978-1-5246-4859-6 (sc)
ISBN: 978-1-5246-4858-9 (e)

Library of Congress Control Number: 2016918421

Contents

Preface ix

1. Arrival on the Dark Continent.............................. 1
2. Arrival in Léopoldville 7
3. First Acquaintances and Introduction to
   Congo Politics... 12
4. Joseph 23
5. First Assignment 27
6. Volkswagen Import and Driver's License................. 31
7. Currency... 34
8. Sports in Léopoldville 37
9. Weekends on the Congo River............................. 40
10. Dysentery 48
11. Gilberte... 50
12. Political Changes 53
13. Social Life and Parties.................................. 56
14. Burglary #1 65
15. Burglary #2... 69
16. New Political Developments 75
17. Stanleyville 77

18. Regional Manager Protemp—Rwanda and
    Burundi 80
19. Arrival in Burundi 85
20. Avenue du Ravin 12 and Handover-
    Takeover of Shell Region Burundi-Rwanda 90
21. First Visit to Rwanda 102
22. Gisenyi, Goma, and Lake Kivu 114
23. Ivan de Stoop and Two Other Belgians
    Taken Prisoner by Uganda Rifles 118
24. Final Days with Paul Bröcker 121
25. Christmas 1964 125
26. Ivan de Stoop's Captivity in Fort Portal, Uganda ... 131
27. Van Oeteren's New Year's Eve Party 136
28. January 1965 139
29. Bujumbura Golf Club—Meeting Mobil
    Oil Manager —Account of Stanleyville's
    Rebel Occupation 143
30. The Rwanda Massacres 147
31. Ita Komanski #1 149
32. Rising Waters of Lake Tanganyika—LPG
    Container Shortage 152
33. Annual Contract Allocation
    with the Rwanda Government 156
34. Ita Komanski #2 159
35. Border Closing Threat between Uganda
    and Rwanda 164
36. From Cyanika to Kampala 170
37. Fort Portal and Queen Elizabeth National
    Park at Lake King Edward 175

38. Visits by Shell Kenya General Manager and Senior Staff 179

39. A Queen's Messenger 182

40. Paraffin Wax Sale to Collège du Saint-Esprit in Kitega 187

41. Communications in Burundi 189

42. Letter from Carola Cutler 192

43. Birthday Celebrations for Mwami Mwambutsa IV 195

44. Final Month in Bujumbura and Return of Paul and Monique Bröcker 202

45. Return to Léopoldville—Assistant Manager Aviation Products.....................206

46. My Next Assignment 211

47. Sale of Volkswagen and Packing Up 215

48. Last Meeting with George de Freitas........217

49. Departure from the Congo 219

Acknowledgments 221

About the Author.. 223

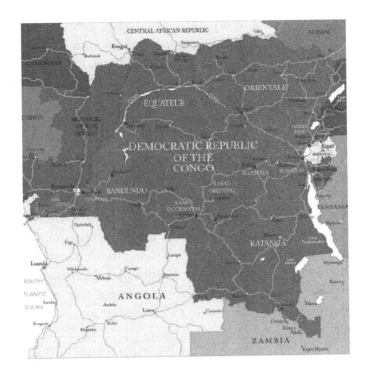

Preface

Several years ago, I decided to put the first pages of this memoir together. The memories of that one year in Africa kept haunting me in such a way that I wanted to get the story down on paper. It was my intention to write it the way I had experienced my life during my stay in the Congo and Burundi. As I mention in this memoir, we did not have a lot of informational resources to verify exactly what was happening in a broader context in the Congo, Burundi, and Rwanda. To weave in the true history of that period, I consulted several of my former colleagues with Shell to be sure that I was accurate about events of that time. I also read several articles in the *New York Times*, which I found in the New York Public Library's research branch on Fifth Avenue. These articles covered the history of the Congo going back to the days of Leopold II. It was also very interesting to read some of the articles covering the time when I was in the Congo and Burundi, especially since a lot of that information did not reach us when it was happening.

In addition, I read several books about the history of the Congo. Fred Wagoner's book *Dragon Rouge: The Rescue of Hostages in the Congo* added to my recollections. The award-winning book by David van Reybrouck, *Congo—Een Geschiedenis* (A History) was an educational experience, as it not only put the Congo into perspective, but added to my own observations and put a lot of what happened there into focus.

I was also assisted by additional information from a variety of sources on the Internet about details of the Congo, Lakes Kivu, and Tanganyika, as well as of the geographical correctness of my travels. It amazed me time and time again how many of the specific stories were still as fresh in my mind as if they had just happened yesterday. However, to make it easier for the reader to refer to specific aspects of events, I have referred to several sources, which can easily be found on the Internet.

Also, note that many of those described in my book are mentioned by their real names; yet, in some instances I have used fictitious names to guard the privacy of some of those I met and mentioned in my story.

1

Arrival on the Dark Continent

The sun rose slowly, and bright-orange light poured into the cabin of the plane. Rubbing my eyes to see better after a night's sleep, I found the morning haze still obscured the view below. As we descended toward the African soil, my excitement rose palpably. I was about to land in Kano, Nigeria, an interim stop on the way to my final destination by plane, Congo Brazzaville. My one year in Africa would begin with a soft touch and a roll.

I walked forward in the plane and stepped through the exit door. Once on the tarmac, the view that had been obscured from above became clearer. I felt wrapped in a dense heat, laden with moisture and many indefinable odors. Decaying vegetation from strange and exotic trees and plants mixed their fragrances; these were the smells of Africa. As if the natural smells were not enough, the fetid odors emitted from a tanning factory on the rim of Kano Airport underscored the decaying land. The wind, blowing from the west, left an even stronger imprint of those smells. These smells would linger with me forever, and now, standing on the tarmac this first day, I was pulled into the mystique of what people called the "Dark Continent."

Decay and rot fighting with sweet fragrances and the lushness of the brush promised a unique year for me, but little did I know how much I would learn about the poles of conflict on this continent. A true learning experience was about to begin for a young man on his first assignment for his first employer, Royal Dutch Shell. It was real; I had landed; the "envelope" opened; I was in Africa!

A year had started, and it would end with another airplane door closing behind me, sealing the envelope in the process. Within this envelope, at the tender age of twenty-three, I would experience the excitement of a foreign land in trouble and in turmoil. I would also experience the intricacies of the oil business through my work: my first year in Africa within the world of Shell. During this time, I would learn to follow instructions and to ignore the same for the benefit of expediency through improvisation. I would be lonely, in love, and loved; I would make friends for life and learn about the fragility of relationships under duress.

Upon joining Shell three months previously in the Netherlands, I never suspected that I would be posted to Léopoldville,[1] the capital of what was then the Belgian Congo, now an independent country. My work assignment wish list had included wonderful-sounding countries where the French language, which I had mastered over the years, could be used: Lebanon, paradise on the Mediterranean; Morocco; or Saigon—but Léopoldville? I never gave it a

---

[1]   During the Mobuto regime, the name Léopoldville was changed to Kinshasa.

thought. So, the dice had been thrown, and here I was heading for this former Belgian colony.

This country was once the private domain of the Belgian king, Léopold II. He had acquired this immense land through a negotiated arrangement in 1885 at the Convention of Berlin. He then ruled and exploited Congo Free State and its habitants until the Belgian Parliament annexed it in 1908, following an international outcry about the atrocities Léopold's forces committed and the loss of life inflicted upon the Congolese population, primarily during the collection of rubber. The Congo was a reservoir of wealth, a land rich with natural resources such as diamonds, timber, palm oil, copper, and many other exotic minerals.

Yet despite the land's riches, the country was poor in educated human resources as well as stable leadership. Since its independence in 1960, Congo Léopoldville was plagued by tribal warfare. I would learn a great deal about the abuse and neglect the country endured under the colonial masters from my colleagues, among them many African hands of long-standing, as well as from my own observations and wise tales told to me by African tribesmen.

After leaving Kano and stopping briefly, we landed in Brazzaville, Republic of Congo, on May 15, 1964. Congo Brazzaville at that time was a uniquely ruled country, as it had adopted the "scientific socialist" philosophy, a term developed by Friedrich Engels following the theories of Karl Marx.

Congo Léopoldville, which like Congo Brazzaville received its independence in 1960, was ruled in a democratic way. In August, a few months after my arrival, the country changed its name to the Democratic Republic of Congo to distinguish it from neighboring Congo Brazzaville, which continued as the Republic of Congo.

This time, when I exited the plane, the wave of heat combined with its unique odors already felt typical, nothing unusual, and just part of the experience of stepping out of a plane in Africa.

Located just south of the equator, Léopoldville has a relatively short dry season that begins at its winter solstice around June and continues through September.[2] The skies are usually gray and cloudy, but hardly any rain falls during this period. The humidity is less than during the rainy season, which starts around the end of September and lasts through the end of May. Temperatures during the rainy season range from the lower thirties (Celsius) during the day, with some cooling, to at best the midtwenties during the evening, while the humidity remains. During the rainy season, blue skies are evident, but rainstorms gather in the late afternoon, and daily downpours are common. An average of fourteen hundred millimeters of rain will fall during that time of the year. The tropical temperatures in Léopoldville are rather constant, ranging between thirty to thirty-five degrees Celsius during the day and dropping to between twenty-five and thirty degrees at night, although during the dry season the temperatures are slightly cooler.

Once again, after reaching the airport tarmac, I walked toward a cluster of gray, austere-looking buildings. We had arrived in Brazzaville, capital of the former French Congo, just across the river from Léopoldville, capital of the former Belgian Congo. The Congo River majestically

---

[2] http://en.wikipedia.org/wiki/Kinshasa#Climate.

separated the two capitals of these countries, which were similar geographically and culturally and but very different politically and economically.

After passing the immigration and customs formalities, our luggage was put on a bus, a weathered and beaten box of steel resembling scrap yard materials back home, a novelty.

Soon I learned that the white man was no longer considered a novelty but was a recognized target for locals to improve their meager lifestyle. "You give; I leave you alone," seemed much embedded in the African mind of the underprivileged. "You don't give, and I will remind you of your failure to share the wealth." The latter, I would experience on a few occasions.

Approaching the bus, a large crowd of natives started to come together and partially blocked us from entering. This ragtag crowd of mostly younger men was dressed in well-worn clothing—mostly just pants and a shirt. Some wore sandals, but most were barefoot and had none of the more colorful clothing worn by a group of women standing aside, holding little children in their arms. The men did not seem willing to let us board the bus. Our driver called out in a booming voice that we should board quickly, and briefly the crowd parted to make sufficient way for the odd-dozen Europeans to clamber aboard. We were barely seated on the rickety upholstered chairs when chants and shouts arose, punctuated by a loud clanging on the side of the bus.

As soon as the door of the bus closed, the crowd started moving closer and closer, their banging on the sides of the bus increasing to a frightening level. The bus started rocking slowly at first but ever perilously faster from side to side. Some of the women started to scream, and a burly, military-looking man pounded his fist next to the driver, imploring him in a commanding tone to start the bus and roll out of this predicament. The driver, with a half grin on his face, complied. The bus coughed to a start, suddenly lurching forward, escaping our antagonists and with increasing speed rolled us toward our next destination. The crowd, which at first attempted to keep the bus from departing, was left in its slipstream; its increasing speed proved to be our salvation.

The narrow escape was a memorable start to my first hours on African soil; it was radically different from the sophistication of my homeland, the Netherlands.

2

Arrival in Léopoldville

A short drive brought us to the ferry terminal bordering the Congo River on the Brazzaville side: a rickety bunch of shacks with a couple of piers that looked as if they would fall apart at any moment. We were urged from the bus by our driver and guided onto a ferry, a real museum piece. We managed to get on board, and with a blow of the horn, the ancient vessel started moving onto the fast-flowing Congo River. The divide between the two Congos, the Stanley Pool, is about three and one-half miles wide and ends to the west with a great series of waterfalls and rapids, the Livingstone Falls.

The Congo River is the deepest river in the world, with depths of more than 250 meters, and at a length of 4,700 kilometers, it is the world's tenth longest river. Below the Livingstone Falls, all the way to the Atlantic Ocean at Luanda, the river is unnavigable, and trains and a road bypass the falls. The river is navigable from Elisabethville (now called Lubumbashi), through Stanleyville (now called Kisangani), all the way to Léopoldville, and steamers ply its fast-running waters to provide transportation for goods and people in both directions.

The open ferry was crowded with some vehicles resembling trucks, a few cars, and lots of people on foot carrying all kinds of bundles filled with merchandise. I noted big bunches of bananas, mangos, and other native fruits including manioc—brown, twisted, root-like specimens—which I had never seen before. As at the airport, the women were dressed in colorful sari-like dresses wrapped around their bodies, and the majority wore turbans of the same or similar materials as their wraps. The men looked shabby, many wearing flip-flops or going barefooted, but rarely did I see regular shoes. A few Africans were dressed in suits and ties, sticking out in this crowd, completely overdressed. They looked official, but I couldn't possibly determine what they were all about. The river flowed fast, but the Stanley Pool was surprisingly empty. A few small craft were progressing on the water in all directions, but I did not notice any larger boats or vessels.

At first it appeared that there was a lot of flotsam on the river, but when some of the bundles floated closer to the ferry, I noted that these were large bunches of hyacinths, some large enough to accommodate several humans. The river was vast and impressive but dark and ominous; the water was not clear, but brownish with a yellowish tint, and I must admit it was not particularly comforting. We chucked along, and it took us about three-quarters of an hour to cross to the border of the Republic of Congo at the Léopoldville harbor.

Upon leaving the vessel, a brief and surprisingly rapid passage through immigration and customs allowed me to move up a ramp, and, at the upper right, I saw a European at least a dozen years my senior, who made a waving motion with his hand. This was my first Belgian boss, Henri Baron van Zuylen van Nijevelt, who welcomed me to the country and to the Societé Congolaise de Pétrole Shell.

After some warm, welcoming words, Henri took me to his home and invited me to stay with him and his wife Monique on this, my first night in the Congo. Henri assured me that the next day we would go to my apartment, owned by Shell, so I could settle into my own abode.

After a nice dinner, followed by a good night's rest, we drove the next morning to the Shell office located on a broad boulevard, the Avenue du Trente Juin, named for the Independence Day of the republic in 1960, but clearly still an homage to the colonial days of the Belgians. The Shell office was a rather modern-looking concrete box of nine floors. The first three floors served as office space, and the remainders were apartments for several of the expatriates.

Although the offices were functional and rather uninviting, my meeting with the various divisional managers, as well as the general manager, George de Freitas, was welcoming. I had been told not to be shocked upon meeting De Freitas, as his face had been disfigured in the Desert War in North Africa during World War II. However, upon meeting him, I found his scars were not too distracting. De Freitas was a very amiable man, and he welcomed me cordially to the company. He told me that Henri would explain my duties during the first two months in the office, which would be followed by a rotation into different positions, temporarily replacing colleagues who would be going on their annual two-month home leave.

After my meeting with De Freitas, I returned to Henri's office, and for the next hour he explained the operations of the Societé Congolaise de Pétrole Shell. As Shell in the Congo had no "upstream" operations, there were no explorations, or refining activities. The company was a "downstream" operation, thus purely marketing and sales. Petroleum products, such as gasoline; aviation gasoline, or avgas; diesel oil; lubricants; and liquefied petroleum gas (LPG) were all imported on import licenses validated through the Ministry of Finance, to allow for overseas payments. These products were bought from other Shell-affiliated companies and transported to the coastal town of Matadi, where they were loaded on trucks and shipped by road to the various Shell depots in Léopoldville. Those products destined for the inland cities were transshipped by road on trucks, where feasible, but mostly by river, loaded on small tankers for the gasoline and diesel products, or on small vessels, in the case of lubricants and LPG.

Shell leased its service stations to local entrepreneurs, provided them with pumps and underground tanks, and local staffs handled the sales and marketing. In addition to Léo, in the larger cities, such as Stanleyville, Elisabethville, Bukava, and a few others, Shell would have one or more expatriates in charge of the local sales operations. Burundi and Rwanda were also part of the Léopoldville-based operations, and one expat was based in Bujumbura to handle all of Shell's business in both countries. In total, Henri explained, we had about twenty-five expatriates in the company, some in sales, others in finance, handling the treasury functions as well as the import licenses and international payments.

Following this first introduction to Shell in Léopoldville, Henri introduced me to the country sales manager, who was also de facto assistant general manager, Edmond Becker. I greeted Edmond in French, the operating language of the company. Upon hearing my fluency in the language, Edmond, a Wallonian Belgian and thus French-speaking, exclaimed, "Finally, London is sending us someone who can speak French!" Apparently, some of my predecessors had not been as fortunate as I was to be endowed with linguistic skills and were sent to Léopoldville without the ability from day one to speak the language fluently enough to be effective in their jobs.

French is the "lingua franca" spoken in the Congo, and the language of all official documentation. It is also used in communication between the various social groupings. Lingala is the main native language spoken between most tribal groups, especially in the west of the country, but Kikongo, Tshiluba, or Swahili are also commonly used, the latter in the east. Thus, Léopoldville is a multilingual city, further linguistically broadened through a great many expatriates. Becker invited me to lunch at his apartment that day. Although I did not know it at that time, Becker would have quite some influence on me during my stay in Léo.

3

First Acquaintances and Introduction to Congo Politics

This first morning at the office, I also had the pleasure of meeting my neighbor to be, Rudolf Bak. Rudolf was sales manager for the Léopoldville Region, an area extending to Matadi, the harbor town on the coast in the east and into the Kasai, the diamond-rich province of the republic stretching to the south and southeast of Léo. Rudolf invited me to dinner that evening at his apartment in our shared villa with his wife Marlies and their two little boys, Mikel and Peter. He also mentioned that the previous occupants of my apartment were a Belgian couple, André and Janine Desmaret, who were on home leave in Europe, hence the availability of the apartment. I would have to move again in a couple of months, after they returned, but Rudolf assured me that Shell had plenty of houses and apartments available. Since I was a bachelor, I should expect a string of moves approximately every two months or so. One of the privileges of being a bachelor was the inevitable flexibility to pick up and relocate! As I transitioned from office to office, I was introduced to a great number of the twenty-five or so expatriates working for Shell in Léopoldville, some of whom you will read about later.

After lunch at Becker's apartment on this first day in Léo, I collected my bags, and Henri took me to a house located on Avenue Lippens, a street named for the former governor of the Belgian Congo of the early 1920s. The house was in a section of town where colonial-style houses dotted the area; it was strictly inhabited by expats and a few high-level government officials. Contrary to some parts of the city, it was well tended, with the lawns mowed and flowers and plants abundantly creating a colorful display in the gardens. The office was about ten minutes away and the riverfront a mere twenty.

We entered a short driveway leading past a grandiose white plastered villa with a large garden surrounding it. Upon entering the building, we climbed a broad stairway to the first floor, where we came upon a huge living room annexed by an equally large dining room. A balcony extended along the front of the building, but it seemed marginally useful as the railing was rather high and the balcony too narrow to lounge comfortably outside.

Having made that quick observation, I was further guided to one of several bedrooms, and Henri suggested that I should use the larger one with an adjoined bathroom. A good-sized kitchen, as well as several large storage areas, complemented the austere dwelling. The rooms were rather dark and were furnished with very utilitarian furniture. I wondered how I was going to take care of this huge place.

Henri came to the rescue! I would have a servant, which he conveniently called a "boy," the lingua franca for a male servant.

The next day, he would bring Joseph to meet me. With Joseph's arrival, my house-cleaning problems would be solved instantly.

Rudolf and Marlies had arrived in the Congo several years earlier and were sent to Bukavu on Lake Kivu in the Eastern Congo. They had been living nearly five years in the house on Avenue Lippens. As it turned out, we would become very good friends, and the Baks helped me enormously to get my bearings, especially during my first weeks in Léo. Their knowledge of the city and the Congo in general would help me to understand the structure and life of this troubled land. Following Rudolf's earlier invitation, I had dinner with him and his charming wife Marlies, the first of many I would enjoy with them. As Shell in London had not exactly provided me with a great deal of information about the Congo, other than a briefing document about the country that was more like a tourist brochure, they brought me up to speed with some basic knowledge about this vast country. They were ecstatic about the beauty of the eastern Congo; Bukavu was located on the southernmost tip of Lake Kivu, bordering the eastern Congo, on the west side of the lake. Rwanda lay on the eastern shore.[3]

Rudolf took some time to explain that the lake was rather unique, as it contained a great amount of CO_2, due to dissolving gas at the bottom of the lake, which is some one thousand feet deep. This gas enters the lake from volcanic rock in this highly volcanic area. In addition to the CO_2, bacteria in the lake convert some of the CO_2 into methane. The combination of these gases causes a special effect, which could lead to a so-called limnic eruption. Although this has

---

[3]   http://en.wikipedia.org/wiki/Lake_Kivu.

not happened in Lake Kivu, the risk of such an eruption, leading to a major suffocating explosion, is always possible. The gases also keep certain animal species away; thus, the lake is free of crocodiles. Rudolf said that swimming there without risk of being attacked by these ferocious monsters had added to the pleasures of living in Bukavu. The methane was mainly on the bottom of the lake and was not harmful to humans, except of course, if it erupted.[4]

I wanted to learn more about the current political conditions and rebellions that were threatening the stability of the country. There was an ever-growing concern that Léopoldville would be the next target for the encroaching rebel armies. Of course, I knew about the most rudimentary developments from newspaper accounts, but what was truly going on was rather obscure.

Although newspapers were scarce, and information about any local or world news was hard to obtain, Rudolf was well informed through his multiple diplomatic and industry contacts, as well as his extended time in the Congo. He reminded me that the Congo had become independent on June 30, 1960. The independence ceremonies had been tumultuous. King Baudouin of Belgium, during his drive from the airport along the main boulevard, had been jumped upon by a Congolese native, who had taken his ceremonial saber and brandished it above his head before he was arrested. Happily, nothing happened to the king, but he had to suffer an embarrassing speech by Patrice Lumumba, head of the Mouvement National Congolais, who proclaimed: "Slavery was imposed on us by force!

---

[4]   Lake Kivu and Methane Gas-http://www.lake-kivu.org/.

We have known ironies and insults. We remember the blows that we had to submit to morning, noon and night because we were Negroes!" The king was shocked and was determined to leave immediately, but his ministers accompanying him persuaded him to stay until later that evening.[5]

Elections were held that very month and saw two prominent nationalists win: Patrice Lumumba became prime minister, and Joseph Kasavubu of the Alliance des Bakongo (ABAKO) Party became president. Within weeks of independence, Katanga Province, led by Moise Tshombe, seceded from the new republic, and another mining province, South Kasai, followed. Belgium sent paratroopers to quell the civil war, and the United Nations flew in a peacekeeping force. Subsequently, to make matters worse for the newly independent country, Lumumba was arrested. Stories conflicted about the way he met his end, but CIA involvement was strongly rumored, as was the presence of Tshombe at his execution. In 1962, Tshombe rejected a national reconciliation plan and, after fierce fighting against the UN peacemaking troops, capitulated in January 1963.[6]

Since late 1963, Rudolph continued, a rebel movement had been growing in the eastern part of the Congo, started as an antigovernment movement formed by former Lumumbist government officials as well as local tribal chiefs. The movement, called the National Liberation

---

5   https://en.wikipedia.org/wiki/Congolese_Independence_Speech.

6   https://en.wikipedia.org/wiki/Democratic_Republic_of
     _the_Congo.

Council, was also backed by the Marxist government of Congo-Brazzaville. The fighters, who were mainly from the Kivu and Oriental provinces, were Marxists. They were led by a Maoist called Pierre Mulele, formerly minister of education and fine arts, together with his comrades Gaston Soumialot and Christophe Gbenye. Apparently, the Chinese, and some Soviet aid, backed the movement, which had already taken over large portions of land in the ill-defended eastern provinces. Mulele had received guerilla training from the Chinese. Soumaliot recruited a lot of supporters, who were very much dissatisfied with the corrupt and authoritarian ways of the central government in Léo.

It had been rumored that many of these recruits for the rebellion were animists who believed that they would be immune to bullets. Their witch doctors predicted that the bullets, when fired at them, would turn to water, leaving them unharmed, and would transform the rebels into *simba*, lions in Swahili. Thus, the name was provided for the rebel movement: *SIMBA*! Rudolf was worried about the advances made by the rebels toward the western part of the Congo. Already, the first signs of rebel activity near Léo had been noted, as recently a railroad in the area had been attacked and blown up.

More attacks were anticipated, and it became clear in the next few days that we were in a danger zone. What a wealth of local news to be absorbed during those first few days in Léo! Surprisingly, it was through word-of-mouth accounts, such as Rudolf's and Marlies' that we would garner information about the political and rebel activities happening in the country. The rumor mill would not be quieted during most of my time there. We prepared at Shell for a potential evacuation of its staff in the event of rebel movement toward Léo.

Despite all these anxieties, social life was thriving in Léopoldville, and the Baks immediately introduced me to plenty of it in town. It had become customary in the expat community to welcome newcomers with a party. Marlies arranged one for my arrival and invited me to their apartment the following Saturday for a masquerade. The guest list included many of my Shell colleagues, as well as expats from several banks both Belgian and English. Among the invited was the general manager of British American Tobacco, Hans Verkerk, a charming Dutchman, fourteen years my senior, who arrived together with his delightful wife, Marian. The Verkerks would become close friends during my stay in Léo. Also present were Jim Don and his wife, Margaret. Jim was the treasurer of Shell Congo, and a dual American and British citizen. I learned later that his father, Kaye Don, was a famous land speed record holder who had a trio of Sunbeam racing cars in the 1920s and had also broken the speedboat world record with the powerboat *Miss England II* in 1931. As with the Verkerks, Jim and Margaret became my close friends during our brief period together in Léo.

Marian Verkerk

It seemed that close relationships were fostered during this time, which could be explained by the intense tension and pressure we all experienced. We had to rely on each other to get things done to make life easier. Just shopping for basic items was a major exercise. This was especially true for the bachelors in our circle of acquaintances, as they were at a great disadvantage to obtain basic household goods such as toilet paper and detergents, as well as beer and soft drinks. To obtain a full case of beer, one first had to acquire a case of empties. Without one, a case of full bottles could not be obtained. It was one of the first things that a newcomer had to do, hunt for an empty case among the expats. It was one of those challenges, but vital! Cases of beer bottles had a special market value, which fluctuated with the needs of new arrivals and the offers made by departing families.

Markets would open in the morning when we were in the office, and if it weren't for the wives of our colleagues and friends, we, the bachelors, could not obtain anything. Available goods would be sold out within the hour after the shops opened. So, my shopping list tacked along with Margaret, Marian, and Marlies, the three *M*s of my grocery supplies!

We expats also spent a good part of our free time together, be it on the golf course or on the tennis courts and, of course, the weekends, where we spent endless hours on a variety of speedboats and other watercraft traveling up the Congo River and into the Stanley Pool. But let me describe my first social event.

As if we had not had enough tension with the rumors of the approaching rebels, the day before the party was held, the government, fearful of ever-increasing incidents and subversive attacks in town by those rebels, declared curfew from six in the evening to six the next morning. It seemed that my first opportunity to meet several people was doomed, but Marlies got on the phone and contacted the invited guests, urging them to bring inflatable mattresses and other sleeping gear. Half of the invited thirty-odd guests did show up, and we partied the night away, with most the group staying until the early hour the next day, while the others bedded down on the floors of the apartment of the Bak family. Marlies had even managed to order balloons for the party, which arrived that very morning from Brussels.

A large breakfast was put in front of this hardy group after this, my first social event, an exciting and unexpectedly great evening and night. It also reaffirmed the necessary closeness we had developed because of the curfew; an additional flow of adrenaline kept us on our toes, guessing what would come next.

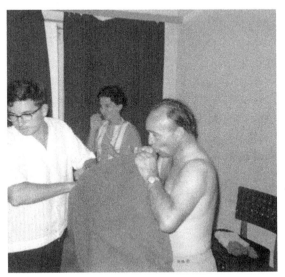

Marlies and Rudolf with guest preparing for an unexpected sleepover because of curfew

The next day, we learned from senior management about an escape plan for the employees of Shell at head office in the event of further rebel activity. The first group of employees would be heading for and trying to depart from N'djili Airport, the international airport of Léopoldville. Several employee and company cars were designated for the escape trip; the cars would be lined up in front of the Shell Building at Avenue Trente Juin. Selected staff members were assigned to drive the cars, and each Shell employee and his family was assigned a spot.

However, since the chances of driving to the airport might well be limited if anything started to erupt, a secondary plan was put into readiness. After a rapid drive to the yacht club, the owners of various boats and I would pilot the boats per a predetermined plan. We labored over a few charts to acquaint ourselves with the fastest and safest route along the Stanley Pool and the Congo River toward a point not too far from the airport. We would land the boats at a certain spot and be guided from there to the airport by some of our African staff, who would be positioned at the place of landfall. Indeed, it was an elaborate plan: fortunately, we never had to implement it.

Speedboat in front of the SHELL cruiser ready to evacuate, but first some fun on the sandbanks!

4

Joseph

Joseph, on the right and colleague

Joseph came into my service on my second day in Léo, having left the employ of a recently departed expatriate family. Henri suggested that I pay the same wages, kind of unofficially fixed by the expats, to avoid causing competition for wage increases among the many expatriate servants. Henry brought Joseph to my house that day after work.

We set out to determine his daily routine. Joseph would arrive at six o'clock in the morning, in time to prepare my breakfast and discuss the daily work to be done around the house. As my houseboy, he was supposed to wash the laundry daily, make the beds, clean the house, and prepare lunch to be served at one fifteen, when I would return from the office. In the afternoon, he would leave around four to return to his house in the Cité, an area of the city primarily inhabited by lower-class Congolese. This trip, I learned, would take him anywhere from a half to one and a half hours, depending on the availability of public transportation, mainly buses, or, more to the point, his ability to pay for the bus.

I found out in due course that the latter was mostly his problem, lack of money, and I soon decided that I would drive him to the Cité from time to time, saving him a lot of time and worry. Joseph, as it turned out, was a very decent cook, and was also available to prepare meals for dinner parties. He would clean after all meals, as part of the duties as a houseboy, but I always made sure to drive him home after a late-night event. Some of my expat acquaintances frowned at my liberal spirit to make life easier for a "houseboy."

Joseph, I guessed, must have been in his late thirties, and was about five feet six inches tall, around the average size for those from his region in the Bas Congo. Like most of his tribal members, he was stocky and broad-shouldered with dark, shiny skin, weathered hands, and he walked barefoot through the house but donned his slippers when he was off to his home. His face was open, and he smiled with a pleasant demeanor like he truly meant to communicate his feelings of pleasure. Joseph was polite; he always confirmed my requests by repeating the tasks I had set out for him to do, and he often asked if *le patron* was happy with the work he had done. Joseph told me that he was married, but I never truly found out the details of his conjugal life, nor the number of children he had. In short, Joseph was a nice chap to have around, who cleaned the apartment with great diligence and, in addition, put quite a good meal on the table.

The apartment of the Desmaret family wasn't in a very clean state when I moved in. Cockroaches roamed at will, and the bathrooms were not exactly spic and span. I had a long chat with Joseph, who, in addition to his native Kikongo[7] and Lingala,[8] spoke excellent French, about the cleaning discipline I would like him to observe during his time with me. Joseph promised he understood, and we turned to the tasks at hand. Water had to be boiled before being used for all cooking purposes, as well as stored in the fridge in carafes. Ice cubes were to be made of boiled water and not taken from the tap directly. I am sure Joseph found me to be overly cautious, but I had been told to be very careful with water issues, especially when cleaning raw vegetables and fruits. Had I only known that liberties would be taken with these instructions, it would have spared me a few bad experiences with my health.

A major task lay ahead for Joseph, but Rudolf assured me, as he was familiar with Joseph's reputation at his

---

7   http://www.kupsala.net/risto/kongo/kituba-english.html.

8   http://en.wikipedia.org/wiki/Lingala.

previous employers, that the job would be done well and thoroughly.

However, at that time I was only hoping that Rudolf's grapevine knowledge was correct about Joseph, because living in Léo without proper hygiene was not exactly my personal cup of tea. So here it was, a few days after my arrival, and I woke up in the middle of the night with a weird itchy feeling on my back. Something was crawling in my pajamas. Slapping myself on the shoulder and turning on the light, I found to my disgust that a huge cockroach had dropped from my back onto the bed, squashed by the impact of my hand. Next day, Joseph was shown the intruder, but it did not seem to make much of an impression other than his promise to follow my instructions for a thorough cleaning of the premises. So much for comfort!

5

First Assignment

Working hours in Léopoldville were set to accommodate the tropical conditions. Six days a week—indeed, Saturdays were still working days—we started at seven in the morning and worked until one o'clock in the afternoon, with a short break for coffee or tea. I rejoiced hearing from Henri about this schedule; it would permit free time in the afternoon for a nap after lunch, which was recommended as a relief from the midday heat. Of course, I wondered at times why we were so concerned about the heat, as the offices were fully air-conditioned, as were our apartments and houses. Nevertheless, such were the rules of the company, and I would not complain one bit about them.

As it turned out, as a junior executive, I was not burdened with an overly heavy work schedule, which allowed me to take full advantage of afternoon sporting activities. I played tennis and golf, unlike my superiors, who would often return to the office in the afternoon to continue their various duties.

PARTY AT SHELL GENERAL MANAGER RESIDENCE

**Hans and colleagues Jim Don second from
right, third from left Arthur Lowthian**

**Hans talking with African colleagues –
Background, Leslie Armstrong –
HR manager talking to colleague's wife.**

In my first ever assignment, I reported to a Belgian national who was the head of a unit that cleared the import licenses through the Ministry of Finance for all Shell's imported products. The bulk of these products were gasoline, gasoil, butane gas, and lubricants. I was responsible for the preparation of the necessary documents to be submitted to the Ministry of Finance, to provide Shell with the foreign currency payment allocations after the various products were imported and cleared. This was rather dull work, but it was part of the process of learning how marketing in the petroleum business operated. In fact, I was being groomed to take over the unit in a few months while my Belgian colleague would be off to Europe on home leave. However, I would only learn this after working a few weeks in the unit. So much for internal communication! It explained my colleague's moderate position in the company as he was approaching his forties. The fact that I, an inexperienced young employee, would replace him was also telling of his lackluster performance.

I was assisted with all this paperwork by a Congolese. This fellow had once been selected to receive special training in Brussels by Belgium Shell, as it was intended to groom him for a senior position in the local company. After a year of training, he returned to the Léopoldville office to receive additional training before he would be assigned to a senior marketing position. An incident that I experienced with him demonstrated why his career had not progressed as anticipated, as he clearly did not have the skills to deal with more responsibility.

One day we were checking the documentation he prepared for the importation of the next shipment of gasoline to Léopoldville, a routine check, which primarily centered on the quantities to be imported. To my surprise, I found the number to be imported as listed by my Congolese colleague amounted to only one million gallons. I called him to my desk and ask him to verify this number, as it seemed that something was not quite right. He looked, and looked again, but he did not indicate that anything was wrong. I knew from previous shipments that the imported quantity had to be ten million gallons. I pointed out to him that the amount was not correct, and I asked him why he had not put the right number in the required box on the import documentation.

He looked at me and, with an expression of great sincerity on his face, said, "But, Hans, the difference is but a zero, so, what is the problem?"

I was flabbergasted, and asked incredulously, "You are joking, are you not!"

"No," he said, "I really don't see a problem."

I just shook my head, made the correction and left the issue alone. Yet I reported the incident to my supervisory colleague, who said, "Now you know why he was not advanced to any senior position and why we needed you to control all these documents closely, just to avoid these kinds of mistakes!" Truly, one wondered what would have happened if this document had been passed on, as the level of capability at the Ministry of Finance office was probably not much better than I just experienced in our office!

Onward we went! No worse incidents occurred, no shipments were delayed or disapproved, and time moved on to my first "promotion," to replace my Belgian colleague when he and his family happily left on their annual two-month leave granted by Shell to all expatriates in these tropical countries.

6

Volkswagen Import and Driver's License

One of the benefits of working for Shell came with the purchase of my first car. Shell allowed for a loan to make this acquisition possible, a total of five thousand Dutch guilders. I went to "Garage Jansen," the VW dealer in Wassenaar, the town I had lived in since 1943, and found a great Volkswagen "bug." The yellowish color was not optimum, but the price was within my budget, so the deal was quickly concluded. Through a moving company recommended by Shell, I had arranged for my personal belongings, as well as the car, to be shipped to Léopoldville.

The shipment took about a month, but during my second week in town, I was advised by Shell's freight forwarder in Léo that my shipment had arrived and that clearance had been undertaken. The next day, a big box arrived at my apartment, and Joseph helped me to unpack my various belongings and put them around the apartment. Now at least I had something of a personal touch in the otherwise rather bleak space of the Shell home.

My car was delivered to the office, and I returned my loaner vehicle to the Shell carpool, grateful that I had been given this free transportation during those first couple of weeks. Traveling as an expat in Léo without a car was impossible, as local transportation was not convenient for trips to the expat housing locations, nor would one gladly venture onto the rickety vehicles that showed age and related wear and tear, amid the hordes of Congolese with their invariable bags, even animals, and "what have you not."

Now in possession of my very first car, I could drive it with my Congolese driving license. I had obtained the license through my colleague Luc Vossen, a burly Belgian expat who was handling the Léopoldville sales district. Luc had ample connections in town, and when I asked him if I should be taking a driving test, or a verbal test of the traffic rules, he broke into a big laugh and told me to simply give him twenty dollars, and within a few days he handed me my license. So, it happened! I never asked Luc details, but he assured me that the license was real and that I had nothing to worry about. So off I went, and happily drove my Volkswagen until a few days before my departure the next year.

I had no idea, nor did I bother at the time to find out, how Congolese obtained their driver's licenses. Although one might have been concerned about conduct in traffic if this was the way a driver's license was obtained, in general, people did not disobey the basic traffic rules, although the traffic could be rather chaotic in town. I personally never encountered any dangerous situations, but then again, traffic was strictly in town on the boulevards or side streets, and the only major highway was to the airport or to the coast. However, few expats went by road to Matadi, the coastal town, so I cannot recount from experience about traffic conditions and related accidents outside of Léo. I had already learned that the Congo was rampant with fraud, and the way I obtained my license was an example of the low level of corruption going on in the country.

7

Currency

I learned a lot about currency manipulation during my year in the Congo. My contract for my first year with Shell stipulated that I would be paid a small amount of my salary in Congolese francs against the official rate of exchange, which at the time was three Congolese francs to one Belgian franc.

This would be used for my local declaration of tax, but I did not have to worry about tax declarations, as the company would take care of that on my behalf. Of course, the local currency allocation was not even 10 percent of my income, which that first year amounted to about ten thousand Dutch guilders. The remainder due to me, after deducting the local currency allocation, was deposited through Belgian Shell in an account at a bank in Brussels that Shell had opened for me. I was told by our HR manager, Leslie Armstrong, a jovial, robust Brit, how we went about obtaining the remainder of any amount we needed to pay for our additional local expenditures more than our local allocation. Simply put, one bought Congolese francs on the black market, usually privately at the rate of about six and a half to seven Congolese francs to the Belgian franc. So, we were benefitting immensely from this opportunity. In fact, we would more than double our local income through this gimmick.

To make the rate even more attractive, our finance manager, Raymond Charrier, would ask the employees their estimated needs for the month, and then he would buy Congolese francs in the millions to be redistributed to us in return for checks in Belgian francs, dollars, or UK pounds drawn on foreign banks. This would increase the black-market rate by at least one more Congolese franc! Expats leaving the country would be selling cars, boats, camping equipment, and other household items, collecting Congolese francs and selling those again at the black-market rate to other expats for hard foreign exchange drawn directly on foreign banks.

Another advantage of this two-tiered system concerned the import of luxury goods to the Congo. A Belgian company made the purchase of caviar, smoked Scottish salmon, whiskey, wine, and other luxury items possible, and provided a wide variety of goods only available to expats. A weekly shopping list could be completed through them, and they would import the goods at the official rate of exchange and subsequently sell to us at those rates in Congolese francs. But since we obtained those francs on the black market, our costs dropped dramatically. To wit, a bottle of whiskey would cost a mere two dollars! I was told a story of a Swiss UN employee who rotated her UN salary, paid in Congolese francs at the official rate, and then rotated the proceeds through the black market. Rumor had it that she had purchased a whole block of apartments in Zurich in just about a year from her profits. Because of all these currency machinations and the way Shell paid us while we were in the Congo, I saved a whole year's salary within my one year's stay, not such a bad haul for a youngster!

8

Sports in Léopoldville

During my early meetings with Rudolf Bak, he told me that Shell provided membership to all expatriates to the Royal Club de Golf de Léopoldville. I had brought my golf clubs, and I was very eager to have an opportunity to start playing again. The club also had several tennis courts, which would be another way to keep up my physical well-being during my stay in the country. The application was a very simple single document, which I was told to submit to the club, whereupon I was invited to present myself to the selection committee. To my surprise, this included Raymond Becker, our sales manager, and two other individuals I had already met on a previous occasion. After just about three questions, I was invited to the bar, and my membership admission was celebrated with a couple of icy cold Primus beers, courtesy of the committee and made by Heineken Breweries' subsidiary Bralirwa, which brewed this beer throughout the Congo.

My first outing at the club was a tennis game with Jim Don. Jim was an excellent player, and my game would not challenge him, yet I tried hard to make it a match.

However, it was not my mediocre tennis that made me surrender to Jim, but the tremendous humidity was enough for me to beg for a break after less than one set. It was apparent how unprepared I was in those first weeks in the dry season.

Fortunately, Shell headquarters and all expat housing were equipped with air conditioners. During my whole time in the Congo, and later Burundi, the electricity never failed; this despite all other things failing miserably in the country. After my first game with Jim, I must admit that I thought I would never again manage to play a game in that humidity, but after a few more tries, also against less formidable players than Jim, I started to find my rhythm, and my body grew accustomed to the weather conditions.

Golf was a whole different story. The golf course was watered naturally, and during the dry season we had to endure a condition of the course that at best could be described as inferior to anything I had been accustomed to in our lowland country in the Netherlands. The greens were made of packed dirt, and it was a completely new experience to try to get the ball into the hole! To play a game without losing balls, due to one's own inability to keep the ball in play, one had to hire a forecaddie, whose job was to protect one's golf balls from disappearing. The balls disappeared from bad hits, but more frequently they were stolen.

Young Congolese would emerge suddenly from the brush after a ball landed not only in the rough, but also on the fairway. They picked up the balls and waited for the player's arrival to demand a reward (a *matabisch* in Lingala) before they would release the ball to its owner. Despite the forecaddies' efforts, it was often that a few francs passed this way into the local economy. Although the course was not exactly a dream, just to be able to go out and play was an additional bonus, better than finding relaxation by hanging around the house in the afternoon. Socializing at the club was also one of the main attractions of membership, and many a tale was told, news gossip exchanged, and beers consumed at the elaborate clubhouse of the Royal!

9

Weekends on the Congo River

Hans on the sandbanks of the Congo River at age 24

Our weeks were long, as we also worked on Saturdays from 7:00 a.m. until 1:00 p.m., but I soon learned that Sundays were the days to escape the humidity and boredom of town. A multitude of expats swarmed to the local yacht club at the edge of the Stanley Pool. A variety of boats would be put into action motoring to the farther reaches of the pool, where a great number of sandbanks had formed in the river. That first Sunday I went with Rudolf and Marlies and their two little boys in a speedy metal craft driven by a 25 h.p. Johnson outboard on our Sunday expedition. The freedom on the water and the somewhat cooler air streaming around us while we sped against the fast-flowing Congo River was a treat.

Large bundles of water hyacinths floated toward the falls, as did logs and other debris stirred up by the river. Rudolf navigated around the floating objects with great expertise, and after a good forty-five minutes, we arrived at a large sandbank, already populated by several other expats. The Dons were present with their flat-bottomed ironclad craft, ideal for landing on the sandbanks. Water skis were already out on the sandbank, and soon Rudolf started to erect a tent to shield us from the sun, although at that time of the year during the dry season, it was mostly reflected light that created a lot of glare. Yet, I was warned that this would cause sunburns and to take precaution with suntan lotion. Food was brought out in big cases, and beer was amply available to create a real picnic outing.

Lounging on the sandbanks of the Congo River

Here in the middle of the Congo River, it all seemed rather unreal, yet one quickly adapted to the relaxed way of life that a weekend trip on the river provided. During my earlier youth, I had learned to be a proficient water-skier. In fact, during my studies in Lausanne, Switzerland, I had been teaching waterskiing during a summer. I had also taught waterskiing after my graduation from high school, when I visited the United States and taught at a girl's camp in Rhinelander, Wisconsin. With that background, it did not take me long to get back in form.

Jim Don proved to be an excellent water-skier as well, and the two of us frequently double skied behind one of the many crafts available to pull us around on the river. Of course, the first time I went on the river, I inquired about the possibility that crocodiles might take an interest in us, especially if we took a fall. I was assured by the experienced crowd that in the middle of the river, the chances of an encounter were virtually zero. Crocs, if around, would be hiding closer to the shores and in the reeds alongside the riverbank.

We never saw one, but one day, the German ambassador fell off his skis and was found dead, presumably drowned. The grapevine reported sometime later that he had apparently suffered a heart attack, which had caused the fall. Whatever had been the case, this was the only fatality attributed to activities on the river during my time in Léo. It was never confirmed that the cause of his death was due to a crocodile attack, but it was suspected due to the mutilated state of his body.

The Sunday outings on the river would have other exciting episodes, such as being pulled through the reeds on water skis by one not-too-cautious Belgian—the same reeds where the crocs where supposed to be. I experienced a harrowing river encounter of a different sort. I, along with a British banker, borrowed the flat-bottomed ironclad boat of Pilou van Nispen, another Belgian expat. We decided to explore the river a bit farther upstream, away from the sandbanks. The ride up the river was like one would imagine exploring Africa. Birds of all kinds flew around us, and the river was narrower at this end of the Stanley Pool, so we could see the contours of the river's edges much better; they were choked with reeds and undoubtedly full of crocs.

I was looking intensely at the movements of the river and detected some unusual turbulence in the water to the right of our boat. I called out to my companion and indicated the whirlpool developing in the water. He did not react, but yelled at me with a horrific shout: "Look ahead; look ahead," I turned my head and saw a huge whirlpool approaching us with the speed of the river's flow. To this day, I don't know why I reacted the way I did, but I rapidly turned the boat to the right, diving headlong into the whirlpool at an angle. I guessed the whirlpool must have been at least ten meters in diameter.

In another inexplicable reaction, I also cut the power of the boat, so the front end dipped into the water at an angle into the now-rising wall of water within the whirlpool. A frightening hissing and burbling sound emerged all around us, but as in a trance I gave full power, and the rear of the boat immediately sank into the edge of the whirlpool, and the powerful Johnson engine powered us across its edge and out of harm's way.

I looked back, and the fast-flowing river took the whirlpool along, and it disappeared. My companion looked ashen gray, sweat pouring from his forehead. He motioned in the direction of the disappearing whirlpool, gasping, "How the hell did you get us out of that one? I thought we were goners!" I guess I must have looked as pale as he did, but after a few minutes, we both calmed down and realized that we had escaped the real possibility of being drowned in the turbulent, fast-flowing Congo River. We returned to the "safety" of our sandbank where, enjoying some cool beer, we reflected about the reality of the dangers on the river. The story certainly did make the rounds, and while we did not feel like heroes, it did warn many of the other boaters to be aware of the river's potential additional dangers besides floating hyacinths and driftwood.

Another episode, which could have ended dramatically, happened when two Englishmen decided to linger on the sandbanks and return to town after most of us had already left for the day. For safety reasons, we always stayed with a group of several boats, just in case engine failure caused a problem in returning to the harbor. On this day, the Englishmen ran their boat into a small cluster of hyacinths floating just under the surface, and their propeller got entangled in the gooey mess, but luckily they were pushed onto a sandbank. Nobody missed them until nightfall, which occurred very rapidly at around six in the evening due to our position near the Equator. Once it was dark, it was impossible to venture on the river to search for the missing men. Thus, it was not until the next day that a rescue party was sent to find them.

They were found, alive, but not too well, as they had been sitting up to their necks in the river to avoid being eaten alive by hordes of mosquitoes ready to feast on this unexpected prey. Both recovered remarkably well, but again the message went out to all boaters to make sure to have a buddy system upon leaving the sandbanks and to never go boating alone.

One weekend, we had two full days for some now-forgotten national holiday. We planned an overnight camping trip on the sandbanks with a large group. Several tents were brought along in addition to our customary equipment usually brought by the Baks and the Dons: mosquito netting, army field beds, inflatable mattresses, pots, pans—everything needed for an extended barbecue, along with crates of beer and demijohns of wine. It turned out to be one big feast! Dancing at night on a sandbank in the middle of the Congo River is not an everyday experience, and jumping across burning campfires was regarded, after the inevitable alcoholic intake, as "the thing to do," consequently followed by extended burns from falls into the hot timbers! But then again, this was the Congo, and we were feasting and forgetting all the tension of Léopoldville for a weekend.

Jim Don relaxing on the sandbanks

Another "fun thing" to do was to go out on the river with our boats and head toward the lights of Léopoldville, the only navigational beacon on the otherwise dark, black river. After a few minutes, one would turn the boat 180 degrees east, back in the direction of the sandbank, away from the lights of Léo. Of course, our eyes would not instantly adjust, and turning the boat this fast would create a total blackness, like hitting a wall, which was the ultimate fun, especially in an alcoholic daze! Soon, though, one's eyes would adjust, and the reflected light from the city would shimmer off the sandbank's edge, providing a guide back to the point of departure.

I was very lucky on one of these nutty boat rides. As I turned my borrowed boat, I came too close to the sandbank and hit a log, or a small piece of debris. My boat instantly came to a halt, and while I tried to put it in forward, then backward, cutting the gas, and putting it in full power, all I heard was the noise of the engine roaring, but there was no movement of the boat. Luckily, I was pushed against the very end of the sandbank by the current, which allowed me to climb out onto the sand. I dragged the boat along the sandbank to the shallow end, where the rest of our group was partying, and anchored the boat for the night. It turned out the next day that the spindle of the propeller had broken, and thus the propeller was just idling and not powering the boat. The next day, Rudolf towed the boat back to the yacht club, and I acknowledged my stupid episode to Pilou, the boat's owner. I don't believe, even after I paid for the repair, that he ever lent his boat to me again!

10

Dysentery

One night in my fifth week, I woke up to find myself on my knees, pressing my head on my pillow, an excruciating pain in my stomach. It was not long before I raced to the toilet and passed a huge volume of diarrhea. Barely able to get back to my bed, I felt like I could drink a river, but after I had just put about two glasses down, I had to race again and managed without damage to reach the toilet for another extensive bout with the ceramic pot. This continued for a few hours, and I knew I had contracted an illness.

At my regular time to get up to go to the office, I called Marlies Bak, and she came immediately to my bedside. No way was I going to go anywhere, and Marlies, who took my temperature, called the doctor that Shell used for all medical attention. I had only been five weeks in the country, but it was clear that despite all my precautions, I had been infected by either an improperly washed salad, improperly prepared water, or who knows what else in this bug-infested land.

Marlies told me that I needed to get a stool sample to her immediately, so the doctor could have an analysis made to determine the cause of my illness. The doctor suspected dysentery and already had prescribed some pills, which Rudolf managed to pick up on his way home for lunch. Meanwhile, my condition was not improving much; the cramps in my stomach were like needles punching outward, and the runs continued. I felt dehydrated, which I was told was normal with any bout of dysentery. The result came back from the doctor confirming that I had bacillary dysentery. I was told to rest, take the pills and drink as much as I could, even if it caused the runs to continue. In addition, I experienced that food was a total abstraction.

With Marlies as my nurse for the next week, I managed to get back in shape, but losing five kilos was not exactly what I had counted on! Although this side benefit did eliminate some of the excess poundage I gained since my Shell training in London, where regular visits to the local pubs for lukewarm British beer had expanded my girth. Again, I was very lucky that my neighbors helped me during this episode. I don't know if I could have coped with this bout of dysentery if I had not been so well cared for by Marlies. I was very grateful for her care, as well as for Rudolf's help to get me to the doctor, when I was finally weaned from the ceramic pot!

As it was, I experienced a repeat dysentery bout a few months later, but although I lost some four kilos at that time, the pains were tolerable, and I got back on my feet much faster. However, having lost much of my intestinal fauna, my system would remain sensitive, especially to spicy food.

11

Gilberte

Meanwhile, the river continued to be a great social gathering place, and every weekend a core group met on the same sandbank. Colleagues who did not have a boat or other members of the extended expat community would be invited along to enjoy a Sunday away from the city and its oppressive heat.

One Sunday, a lovely young lady joined one of our regulars, a Swiss diplomat and his wife. She was about my age, a brunette with a stylish bikini and apparently single. Of course, I had no idea if she was single, but it appeared that she was alone. In Léo this would not mean necessarily that she was not part of the married crowd, as some husbands had to travel to the interior of the country, or to Matadi on business, and were often away for a few weeks at a time. I slowly made my move, and before long, we were introduced by the Swiss couple.

Her name was Gilberte, and she was the secretary of the Swiss ambassador. As she had nothing planned for that Sunday evening, as if there was a lot going on in town anyway, she accepted my invitation for an early dinner. She had been a few months in Léo, living alone in an apartment provided by the Swiss government.

We had an instant infatuation, and the fact that I had studied at the University of Lausanne in Switzerland made it easy to find discussion points. That evening at dinner, it did not take much to convince her to meet again.

On my second date with Gilberte, we went out on the town to the Belgian steak restaurant to sample the excellent steak tartar. Our discussions were easy, flowing from our backgrounds in the Netherlands and Switzerland, converging on my studies in Lausanne, which had given me knowledge of the history of her native country.

She was a pleasant young lady, a bit self-effacing, yet very correct and protective of her position as the secretary of the Swiss ambassador. Of course, she was privy to much more information than most of us expats could obtain, but she was very careful not to reveal more than tidbits, mostly enhancing stories that were already circulating. She did confirm the severity of the rebel activities taking place in the east of the country and the apparent horrors committed by the Simbas, which included a lot of killings of foreigners, as well as priests and nuns. It was gruesome, and hearing her confirmation did not give us any comfort about the potential that these rebels might move forward to Léopoldville.

To relax further and get away from such an intense discussion, we followed our dinner with a visit to one of the few nightclubs frequented by foreigners. Great Congolese music was featured, and we could dance, increasingly more intimately, encouraged by a hefty intake of local beer. It was not difficult to persuade Gilberte to join me that night in my bungalow. For the next few months, she moved in with me. Our relationship was great, close and sexual, as we were both young and active. During those months, together, she was my partner at most of the social events, and we were invited as a couple, yet the relationship, while close and full of tenderness, did not seem to escalate beyond an infatuation. However, it also kept me out of trouble, as I was hitched to her and not tempted to get into the morass of problems some bachelors appeared to have gotten into with some of the married women in our expat community.

12

Political Changes

Meanwhile, the political situation had taken some dramatically new twists. The rebel activity Rudolf had mentioned earlier was now in full expansion. The rebels were now calling themselves the National Liberation Army (ANL, French abbreviation) and had captured several towns in late July, including Baudouinville and Kindu.

During this time, our colleague, André Desmaret, who had the apartment above the Baks, where I stayed, had returned from home leave and reoccupied the apartment. However, he was immediately reassigned to Stanleyville, and it was through his dispatches to De Freitas that we learned about the developments in the middle of the country.

Stanleyville had been a stronghold of Lumumba, who was murdered in 1961, and the Simba rebels from the Katanga area who were still loyal to him captured the city in early September. The Congolese army had fled and left their armaments, further reinforcing the Simbas, who were now moving north and west of the city. The central government was supported by the US government, and with the ever-spreading threat of the Simba rebellion, they decided to recall Moise Tshombe, who in 1960 started the breakaway of the province of Katanga, the copper-rich province in the southeast of the country. After this rebellion failed, Tshombe had gone into exile and was now recalled, providing a sense of national unity. He was sworn in on July 9 as the new prime minister.

The United States had agreed to back Tshombe in recruiting foreign mercenaries, and expanded his airstrike force. Tshombe brought in Major Michael Hoare, later better known as "Colonel Mad Mike." Hoare was notorious for building a mercenary force primarily recruited in South Africa and Rhodesia. He was an Englishman, born in India and raised in Ireland. He had moved to South Africa and became well known due to his incursions in the eastern Congo, fighting the Simbas and routing them in some brutal battles. Mike Hoare apparently was the ideal leader of the mercenaries, soft-spoken, cool and collected, and every inch a true English officer and gentleman.[9] Much more news was not reaching us at our level, but we were aware from the dispatches from Stanleyville that the situation was deteriorating rapidly.

Life in Léopoldville was tense, but this did not affect us too personally, although it was true that we were being drawn ever closer to the rebellion. One day, just a day after I had been dining with a few people in the garden of a well-known local restaurant, a bomb was thrown into that

---

[9]   http://www.mercenary-wars.net/biography/mike-hoare.html. Source: *Mercenary*, by Mike Hoare, published by Robert Hale in 1967.

very garden. I had been lucky! However, Tshombe ordered curfew to be changed, so we could be outside between 6:00 a.m. and 10:00 p.m. This change was a great relief for many, as it allowed a little more time in the evening to go out for the ubiquitous parties, of which there were sometimes as many as three in an evening. A few months later, curfew was extended to an even later hour and no longer disrupted our lives to any great degree.

Several incidents affecting expats had taken place during the earlier days of curfew. The secretary of the British ambassador, who was a regular on our Sunday Congo river outings, had been arrested by the police when she was only a block away from her apartment; the police said it was past six o'clock. It had been a quarter to six, but Congo time was not always in sync, hence she was carted to a police post and put in custody. She made a real ruckus apparently and demanded to make a call to the ambassador. Her request was granted, and she was personally escorted out of the police post by the ambassador himself, who had driven to the post to demand her release under diplomatic immunity.

On another occasion the police arrested an expat because his kids were carrying plastic toy guns in the car. They also were ultimately released after some diplomatic intervention.

13

Social Life and Parties

Social life in Léo was very active; any reason to celebrate was a reason to celebrate. In addition to birthday parties, we received invitations to farewell parties for those going on home leave, or for those returning from home leave. Then you had the permanent farewell parties and the welcoming parties, as I had experienced upon my arrival.

A certain mix of people was invited. The Belgians had their party group, and they would not necessarily mingle with the expats from the banks, Unilever, British-American Tobacco, and Shell; a selected group of diplomats would join this group as well. How it all worked was never completely clear to me, but it just happened. The groups developed close relationships, which would include lunches on those days that we would not go to the river, and there were quite a few kids who would be part of the fun. Dinner parties could be extended events. I gave my first party when I moved into my second residence, a large colonial home occupied by our finance manager, Raymond Charrier, who had asked me to move into the house for the period of two months when he and his family would be on home leave. Charrier had put all his personal belongings in a small guest room and locked this with double locks. Lucky for him that he had taken this precaution, as will be told later in this tale.

**The Home of Charrier and my second
residence in Léopoldville**

Home leave was a two-month vacation granted after one year in service in the Congo. As this country was on the list of dangerous countries, we were not only given "danger allowances," but also this yearly two-month vacation privilege. In addition, each year spent in a tropical country earned three months' earlier retirement with a maximum of five years. As such, a Shell employee could theoretically retire at the age of fifty-five, five years earlier than the official

Shell retirement age of sixty, if sufficient tropical years had built up.

I had planned a party for my twenty-fourth birthday on August 6, in part to celebrate the event, but also as a "thank you" for the many invitations I had received during the first months of my stay in the Congo. Making the guest list proved easy, and yet it was also my first encounter with the difficulty of being a rather junior Shell employee trying to select some senior people to invite to a party. It was easy to invite those who had invited me in the past. Yet, I was a rather social guy, and I have never been too concerned about rank. If people I liked were willing to come to my party, I saw no reason not to invite them.

During my various trips on the river, I had an opportunity on several occasions to go with George de Freitas, our general manager, and his elegant and charming partner, Victoria. She, by the way, was something else, always immaculately dressed even in tropical heat and often accompanied by her Siamese cat, which she kept on a rather exotic leash. I liked George and Victoria. On a few Shell occasions, I had been to their residence, a huge colonial mansion with extensive gardens, but never had I been invited personally to a more intimate event. Yet I saw no reason not to invite the couple, and to my delight and some surprise, they accepted. Little did I know that this would put a lot of bad blood between me and Edmond Becker, the sales manager and de facto assistant general manager. I had not invited him, or any of my other Belgian colleagues, except Henri van Zuylen and his wife and Luc Vossen and his wife. I liked Vossen; after all, he had obtained my driver's license.

I had arranged with a Dutchman to move his piano to my home for the party. Peter van Osrand was earning a living peddling mutual fund shares to the expat community for Bernie Cornfeld's Investors Overseas Services, the then famous "Fund of Funds."[10] In addition to being a very good salesman, and hence a star producer for Bernie, he also played the piano very well and had agreed to do so at my party.

Dinner in the garden of my residence

---

10   http://en.wikipedia.org/wiki/Bernard_Cornfeld.

Dancing at full throtle

Line dancing in Africa

Friends avoiding a dip in the pond!

My personal "chef," Joseph, would regale us with an extensive pasta buffet, and for starters, another Dutchman had offered to make a cocktail of crocodile meat! The latter I had never tasted, but he assured me that it would be a bit like a crab cocktail with appropriate sauces laced with the local *pili-pili*, a potent pepper, and very much in style with our local cuisine. Indeed, the proof was in the tasting! Although a little tougher in texture than I expected, the combination with a great cocktail sauce was an unexpected winner. Joseph also concocted a delicious dessert, so my dinner was well received; the music played and the liquor flowed, all in grand style.

This August evening was warm, humid, but not unpleasant, and my driveway, as well as the garden, was lit by torches; brown shopping bags one-third filled with sand to anchor a candle provided a romantic glow. I must say that the evening proved to be a success and was widely praised by those attending.

Obviously, the presence of De Freitas with his Victoria was noted and rapidly the buzz went through the company that this Dutch youngster had dared to invite the general manager to a party, but without consulting other senior staff and omitting to invite other senior managers as well. Of course, it was my take that I was throwing a private party to which I was at liberty to invite whomever I wanted. Indeed, this was a naïve observation of a politically untrained youngster, but heck, I enjoyed a glorious birthday party and learned the consequences later.

Parties had another cause and effect. During curfew, many couples partied the time away in the Shell Building, where, as I have mentioned before, six floors were occupied by some very large and some smaller apartments. Personally, I was never invited to any of those events, except for a few lunches, but it was widely rumored that these parties resulted in a few divorces and separations due to the apparent availability of too much alcohol and some very sexually active employees. One wife apparently had a reputation as a nymphomaniac and was available at any time, at home or wherever. This kind of atmosphere seemed also to be engendered by the tension of the times. Also, jealousy in some instances played havoc with relationships. In my group of acquaintances, some extramarital activities were rumored, but I did not witness any inappropriate behavior at any of our events.

In addition to our dinner and other parties, we had a weekly poker group, rotating from home to home and playing for low stakes. It became tradition that the host's wife would prepare a meal, the host would dole out the beverages, and play would end before curfew started. We played every Wednesday, occasionally inviting some new "prey," although this would backfire from time to time when we discovered the astuteness of the invitee, who would walk away with a fair take of the evening's stake. Yet these evenings further consolidated our friendships; they offered an opportunity to exchange more tales and rumors in an otherwise stale environment for real and confirmed news.

We also arranged numerous classical music evenings. The host would preselect several records from well-known artists, and we would again gather with a select number of our friends and acquaintances to sit quietly and listen to concerts produced by record players, as if we were in one of the great concert halls around the globe. It provided a modicum of cultural awareness and activity that we were otherwise deprived of in this town. Yes, there were a few bars and some very good restaurants, but other than a few occasions, we did not go out too much on the town. Just for the record, one restaurant, which was run by a chef from Brussels, provided excellent steaks, and even a mean steak tartar! One wondered where they obtained their high-quality beef, so one evening, I asked the chef, and he told me that the steak came from South Africa, flown to N'djili Airport, where he collected the shipment of meat himself. A proper amount of *matabish* made the customs facilities cooperate, and the fact that the meat came from the apartheid country was irrelevant, if the chain of providers, including those at customs, would be making a buck!

Time progressed rapidly during those first months in Léo. My first job had already come and gone, as I had replaced my Belgian boss during his two-month home leave. He was about to return, and Luc Vossen was about to go on his home leave, when I was told that I would have to replace Luc during his absence as the sales manager for the Léopoldville District. As it turned out, this was more of a supply and distribution job, making sure that our client owners of the Shell gasoline stations were properly supplied from our various depots. The contracts were rather straightforward, and Luc had left a very good administrative office for me to manage. It turned into a rather routine and not very exciting period without much of a chance to demonstrate personal capabilities. I kept my head low and managed the job.

14

Burglary #1

The wealth disparities in Léo were apparent: the expats and Belgian merchants, as well as the upper-class Congolese businessmen and government officials, lived in the well-to-do suburban areas in large colonial-style villas, or more modest bungalow-style homes protected by gates and tropical vegetation and the inevitable guards at night.

The latter were supposed to be a deterrent for would-be burglars. Clearly, these residential areas were a natural target for burglaries and other kinds of assaults on individuals and property. It was known that for a few francs, the guards would turn their attention away from their protective duties. Often, one would come home and find the guards fast asleep somewhere on the property, and only by flashing one's lights, or honking the horn, would they appear and open the gates. Such was the case when one American diplomat returned home one night and saw his guard in the back of the garage lying on a table, seemingly asleep. No amount of honking or headlight flashes managed to get him to open the gate. The diplomat left his car, walked to the guard, and made an appalling discovery: the guard had been cut to pieces with a machete. The house had been burglarized and very effectively emptied of most of its possessions! It was rumored that the diplomat and his family were transferred to another post.

One Sunday, I returned in the late afternoon from an outing on the Congo River. I was still living at the Charrier home, and driving down to the garage in the back of the property, I glanced toward the back of the house and noted that one of the doors to the terrace was standing open.

Immediately, I realized that the house had been entered and that a robbery might still be going on. Not wishing to take any chances, I backed out of the property and raced to the Shell Building to alert Leslie Armstrong, who had been on the river trip with me. I felt that the personnel manager was the best equipped to stand with me; in addition, Leslie was a big fellow.

Perhaps I should have entered the house, but I had been warned by colleagues not to ever be the hero, as it was not uncommon for burglaries to turn bloody. Leslie joined me in my VW, and we raced back to the house.

We entered through the open door, and it was very apparent that I had disturbed the intruders, as a large pillowcase was lying in the middle of the room still partially filled with clothing and other items. Meanwhile, I noted several of my possessions were missing: no more radio, no more typewriter. We entered my bedroom and saw that a large amount of my clothing had been taken, and other items were on the floor.

The bedroom used by the Charriers as a storage room had not been opened, but the intruders had tried to force the lock, and the trimming of the door had been partially destroyed where they had tried to pry open the door. Since we could not repair the terrace door that day, Leslie offered to let me stay at his apartment, a gesture I greatly appreciated.

The next day, Leslie told me that De Freitas had suggested that I take his driver and car and go to the Cité to visit the various native markets to see if I could find any of my clothes offered for sale. Of course, while the thought was well intended, despite scouring a half dozen partially hidden markets, all I experienced was a near tourist view of the local culture and the variety of wares offered. This alone compensated for the loss of personal property. I don't think a white person without the guidance of a local Congolese would have ever found some of these markets, let alone could have walked around undisturbed through the throng of natives.

Shell compensated my losses, paying me in Belgian francs deposited in my bank account in Brussels, but replacing my typewriter, radio, and cassette player was not possible, simply because these items were not available for sale, and neither were the clothes I had lost. I was glad to still have enough clothes to pull me through to the next event, which occurred a few months later.

Charrier and his family returned, and I had to move again. This time I went to an area called Parc Hembise, a suburb some fifteen minutes from the center of town, quite a hilly area with lots of palm trees and several comfortable bungalows with small gardens, nothing like the Charrier house, but very cozy with plenty of space for a bachelor. Joseph stayed with me, as he had at the Charrier house, and his first task was to give the house a thorough cleaning. I had learned that a clean house at least minimized some of those atrocious cockroaches from taking over the property.

I settled in my third home since arriving in the Congo. I was very lucky to have as my neighbors Jim and Margaret Don, who had a larger bungalow across the street. Another delightful expat couple, the McLarens and their kids, he a banker with one of the British banks, also lived in the area and made this latest move very palatable. We would have a great time during my next two months in Léopoldville.

15

Burglary #2

It was at this house, Parc Hembise 4, that I was burglarized a second time. After an evening with the Don family, I walked back across the street and saw my guard sitting at the gate, as usual with a very sleepy face, but otherwise he seemed undisturbed. Upon entering the house, I felt that something was wrong. After I had been burglarized the first time, I had borrowed a radio, which was gone from the desk in the main room. I raced through to the toilet at the back of the house, where the normally closed door was wide open; the window was wide open, and the iron burglar bars had been bent apart. Clearly the burglar, or burglars, had entered through this window and rummaged through the house.

Electronic equipment, money, and especially clothes were mainly their target. So, it was that I was left with my pajamas, which they had not located behind the bathroom door, a few pairs of socks, my underpants, and one shirt. After taking initial stock of the damages done, I ran back to the Dons' house and related the latest incident.

Jim immediately got on the phone to the police, full well knowing that this was a fruitless effort, but one never could tell how they might react. Now I witnessed a hilarious interchange between Jim and a police officer at the station.

Jim: "I'd like to report a burglary."

Officer: "A what?"

Jim: "A burglary. They broke into the house of my neighbor."

Officer: "Which house?"

Jim: "Parc Hembise #4."

Officer: "Which park?"

Jim: "Parc Hembise."

Officer: "What are you reporting in Parc Hembise?"

Jim: "As I said to you before, a burglary. There were thieves in the house. They stole a lot of goods. Would you send some officers?"

Officer: "Send what?"

Jim: "Would you send some officers to view the damage and take stock?"

Officer: "Take what? They took what?"

Jim: "No, I'd like you to come to take stock of the situation."

Officer: "What situation?"

Jim: "Please, I repeat again: there has been a burglary, and we need you to come out to check out the situation, the break-in, and the losses."

Officer: "Yes, I understand now. Where are you located?"

Jim: "Parc Hembise, you know the suburb?"

Officer: "The what?"

Jim: "You know, Parc Hembise, the residential area?"

Officer: "Ah, you mean Parc Hembise."

Jim: "Indeed. When can you come out to the house?"

Officer: "Perhaps in an hour?"

Jim: "Why does it take that long?"

Officer: "We only have one car, and they are out to check some disturbance. The other cars are broken."

Jim: "What is your name so I can make a note I talked to you?"

Officer: "Why do you want my name?"

Jim: "To be able to recall that you talked to me tonight about the burglary."

Officer: "Yes. You talked to me tonight about a burglary. We will be there in about an hour."

Jim: "Much appreciated, but what's your name, officer?"

Officer: "Olivier, *patron*. We will see you later. If we are not there in an hour, call back!"

Jim: "Thank you, Olivier."

Officer: "You mean me?"

Jim: "Yes, officer, let's end the conversation."

Officer: "Yes, *patron*, but what is the address again?"

Jim: "One more time, Parc Hembise #4. You know where that is?"

Officer: "Yes, *patron*, your address has been noted, and you'd like us to come to see the burglary!"

Jim: "Yes, Olivier, let's leave it at that. *Au revoir et a bientôt!*"

Jim hung up, and we were roaring with laughter. It was a good relief to have gone through this comic exchange. Of course, it had been conducted in French, and the translation doesn't exactly reflect its true content. Believe it, or not, the police did show up an hour later. First they visited the house and observed the scene, and I joined them behind the house where the yard was, now bathing in the outdoor lights I had turned on. We found a broken pole from the laundry stand in the garden that the burglars had used to force the bars of the toilet window aside. They must have been very small persons, able to wriggle through the narrow space left between the bent bars.

One of the police officers tracked some footprints left in the dirt behind the house, and as he proceeded along the narrow path that led away into the brush, he shouted at me triumphantly: "Master, come look, I have found some papers." Believe it or not, spread on the ground I found my address book, some unimportant notes, but, importantly, my Dutch passport, completely intact!

To underscore their authority, the police arrested my guard, despite my protestations, and took him to the police station. They also wanted the name of Joseph, as they said that often a houseboy initiated these crimes. Although I assured them that Joseph had my full trust, they showed up the next day early and arrested poor Joseph before I could stop them. Later that day, both Joseph and the guard returned, bruised and shaken, as they were given a going-over at the police station with truncheons and fists. Of course, neither had anything to do with the crime, but I did give the guard a real talking to for the fact that he had not noticed anything.

I could not prove that he had been asleep either, and I was sure that the policemen would have extracted any cooperative activity from him. It was a very emotional situation; Joseph told me that the police had no respect for their compatriots, especially if they are not of the same tribal affiliation. This is how I learned more about the personal brutality exercised by local authorities. It confirmed in a very small way the massive killings and brutal treatment that was rumored to take place in the area controlled by the rebels in the eastern and middle Congo.

Many assaults, break-ins, and robberies occurred in and around Léopoldville, and we would learn about them with increasing frequency.

One occurred at the house of a wealthy Dutchman I had recently met. His family had moved to the Congo after they had fled Indonesia during the exile of Dutch nationals in the fifties. They once owned a major cookie manufacturing company in Java, and upon arriving in the Congo, they restarted the same business. One of their main contracts was to provide cookies to the Congolese Army. I was shown some of this product, and for the life of me, I could not eat any of them because they were so hard that my delicate Dutch teeth could not bite even a small piece into edible sizes.

In any event, this chap had several places where he maintained sales offices, one in Coquilhatville, some 150 kilometers to the north of Léo. Once a month, his managers would come to visit him and pick up the cash to pay their employees. One day when the pickup was made, two police officers arrived at his door and demanded to enter the house to check some papers. As they entered, they drew their guns and forced the Dutchman and his manager, a Frenchman, into a lavatory on the ground floor and proceeded to go through the house to search for the money. Obviously, they had been tipped off about the monthly pay situation.

While they were rummaging through the house, the Dutchman and his companion managed somehow to break the window and the screen of the lavatory's window and, one after the other, they jumped out. The Dutchman, a large, rotund fellow, had trouble wriggling through the small window, but luckily for him, as we were told, he just fell to the ground and started running from the house.

One of the fake police officers entered the toilet, jumped on the toilet seat and started shooting at the two. While zigzagging through the garden, they managed to find their way out without being hit by the flying bullets. The next day, through some snitching by some of the locals, the police found the two robbers, and the police recovered the money. The Dutchman was summoned to the police station, and when he entered the room where the two robbers were held, he witnessed Congolese police brutality executed on these two fellows. He recalled later that he had never seen such violence exercised with clubs and rubber truncheons. The police were beating them to pulp, while trying to extract information about their other companions and informers.

Once again, through these witness accounts, I learned about the terrible cruelty that occurred in this country for even minor infractions. Respect for fellow citizens was a rarity. Individuals who personally benefited through corruption, cruelty, and ignoring basic human rights were the primary drivers of society in those days in the Congo.

16

New Political Developments

By mid-1964, the rebel forces of the Committee National de Liberation (CNL) held two-thirds of the Congo, and it became clear that something had to happen, otherwise, the CNL and its ragtag bands would take control of the whole country.

Prime Minister Moise Tshombe, appointed by Kasavubu in July of 1964, attempted to contact the rebel leadership of the CNL.[11] However, his final attempt in Bujumbura to meet with one of their leaders was unsuccessful. Since the leadership of the CNL was much divided, Tshombe's attempt to gain regional support in Stanleyville was equally unsuccessful. We learned that Stanleyville had fallen to the rebels of the CNL on August 5. At that point, we heard that Colonel Michael Hoare, who had been recruiting mercenaries in South Africa, started a countermovement by attacking Albertville with a small group of his men across Lake Tanganyika. The mercenaries were now fully engaged,

---

[11]   http://en.wikipedia.org/wiki/Congo_Crisis.

and their actions would ultimately prove decisive for routing the CNL. However, in Léopoldville, we learned relatively little about the details of the ongoing military actions in the eastern Congo.[12] Yet, because of the increasingly successful activities of the mercenaries, Tshombe changed the curfew from twelve hours, 6:00 p.m. to 6:00 a.m., to 11:00 p.m. until 6:00 a.m.

---

[12]   http://www.mercenary-wars.net/congo/index.html.

17

Stanleyville

Following his return to the Congo from home leave, my colleague André Desmaret was immediately appointed regional manager for the Stanleyville area. He could not have been sent at a worse moment. The town had been under control of the rebels since August 5 and had witnessed a degradation of an already low level of discipline in the so-called Armée Nationale de Libération (ANL), which was made up of the notorious Simbas.

As we had heard already, the Simbas believed that if they doused themselves with water, *mai* in Swahili, they would be impervious to bullets. Hence, they would sway and dance and wave wetted fly swats around to stay wet, all the while singing "Mai Mulele" in veneration of one of the key leaders of the ANL. They were also drugged with *dagga*, a form of marijuana, while they pursued their conquests of villages, murdering whites and raping women in the process. After the rebels captured Stanleyville, the Congolese Army fled the city and left large amounts of armaments that the Simbas used to further penetrate the west and the north. At one point, they were reported to have taken Lisala, a town well west of Stanleyville on the way to Léopoldville.

Reports about acts of violence and terror by the ANL soldiers against whites and tribes in the captured territories were reaching us daily. But now Tshombe's efforts to regain the upper hand in his fight against the ANL were succeeding with his forces bolstered by the mercenaries, who provided much-needed officers and leadership.

A two-pronged advance, one along the Ugandan border toward the northern cities of Bunia and Paulis, and a second toward the rebel capital of Stanleyville, was succeeding. Christophe Gbenye, a former minister of the interior in the government of Lumumba and now the self-declared president of the People's Republic, the territory captured by the Simbas for the Committee National de Liberation (CNL), announced in response, in a broadcast on November 6, that he had taken sixty Americans and eight hundred Belgian citizens as hostages. He took this action to prevent further moves against his position in Stanleyville, threatening also that he could not guarantee the properties and the lives of those taken hostage.

Horror stories, already circulating from other parts of the Congo taken by the rebels, started to be heard in Léo. On November 16, a broadcast announced that an American medical missionary, Dr. Paul Carlson, would be executed as a spy. Nobody believed any of Gbenye's pronouncements, but it was evident that he was serious about using the hostages in his defense of Stanleyville. André Desmaret, our Shell colleague, was rumored to have been taken hostage as well, but none of this was confirmed.

Only after my arrival in Bujumbura, as further explained in the next chapter, did we receive a message from head office that indeed André had been held hostage but had been saved, although badly traumatized. He was flown to Belgium for an extended period of recuperation from the ordeal. Dr. Paul Carlson did not survive, as he was killed by the Simbas on that very last day before the Belgian parachutists liberated Stanleyville.[13]

13   Beloved Dr. Paul Carlson, http://www.belovedadventurer. com/2011/06/dr-paul-carlson.html.

18

Regional Manager Protemp— Rwanda and Burundi

Meanwhile, my career with Shell was about to take a major turn, because of the ongoing developments in Stanleyville. I received a call from De Freitas's Dutch secretary, to come see the boss in his office at once. I was quite surprised, as I had only met De Freitas on social occasions, including my controversial birthday party, as well as during the weekend outings on the Congo River. De Freitas did not waste much time introducing me to the problem he was facing in Burundi and Rwanda.

Paul Bröcker, a Dutchman in his early forties, had been the regional manager for a few years and was due to go on home leave in early December for three months. André Desmaret was originally assigned to temporarily replace Paul, but had been caught in the terrible hostage situation in Stanleyville, so De Freitas told me: "Hans, you are the one to go to Bujumbura to replace Paul. Paul will brief you on the company both in Burundi and Rwanda for about three weeks, then you will be managing our interest for the next three months. Upon Paul's return, you will hand back the company to him."

My astonishment must have been quite clear to De Freitas, because he continued immediately: "I realize full well that you have only been with the company for six months here in Léopoldville and that you have relatively little experience in managing an operation. Mind you, it is a small operation with some twenty-seven employees in Burundi and a few more in Rwanda, but Shell will find out what you are made of, and I count on you to show your mettle. If it all goes well, which I expect, you will be on your way to a fine next position in the company. However, if for some reason it turns out to be a mistake, well, Shell will not notice much of a difference!"

After those telling words, I returned to my office to reflect on this much-unexpected situation. I realized, though, that an important opportunity was being thrown my way.

Where else would a twenty-four-year-old be given such a chance? I was quite honored, but I knew that this was a break for me due to terrible circumstances for one of my colleagues, André Desmaret, who now was still held hostage by some savage group of rebels in the middle of a brutal situation.

As it happened, this message was delivered to me only a few weeks after I had been burglarized a second time in my home at Parc Hembise. I had written to my parents to send new clothing, as it was impossible to buy any in Léo. I had many last-minute tasks, such as finding a temporary home for my boat, which I had purchased from the Baks upon their departure on leave and onward to their new Shell assignment, as well as my car. Ultimately, I loaned both to a British banker.

Finally, I packed my belongings and stored them at the Shell office. Indeed, I would leave the country with only one suitcase containing toiletries and clothing given to me by friends and colleagues. I rushed another letter to my father with the latest news of my temporary assignment, together with instructions to send my clothing to Bujumbura. My parents had moved to Brussels a few years earlier, where my father had joined the European Investment Bank as their general counsel, and a Brussels connection made it a lot easier to get things shipped to me in Burundi. At my suggestion, he contacted Belex-Congo, which was moving goods to Bujumbura on regular flights directly from Brussels, to make sure that my clothing would be delivered shortly after my arrival. The latter had been ordered from Wulfsen & Wulfsen, a renowned store in The Hague specializing in tropical clothing. I had bought my initial tropical outfit at this place, including a white tuxedo, which I thought I might use at some point. These clothes had to be replaced, but since W&W had all my measurements, the replacement order went very quickly and was sent to my father in Brussels, who subsequently shipped it to Bujumbura.

In addition, I put together a briefing program with my colleagues in sales, distribution, and human resources, and gathered as much information about my new job as I could. I also made sure I understood the reporting lines in my new job. As it turned out, I would have several direct lines of reporting, above all with De Freitas, who told me that he wanted me to send him information, in writing, about the local political and economic situation, to the extent I could obtain this. In addition, I would report on sales to Becker, and to Charrier's department on operations matters regarding purchases of equipment. It became quite clear that most the business was conducted in Bujumbura and that the regional manager would have a lot of autonomy. Communications would be by telex and phone.

I learned that our supplies for Burundi were shipped from Kenya to the port town of Kigoma by rail and further transported by barges to Bujumbura across Lake Tanganyika. The supplies for Rwanda arrived by truck from Kampala in Uganda. Paul Bröcker would explain further details to me upon my arrival in Burundi during a two-week "handover-takeover."

Jim Don was also quite helpful regarding some aspects of the treasury activities. He also told me a bit more about Paul Bröcker, of whom he did not have a high opinion. Apparently, Paul was a rather volatile chap who had visited Léo before I arrived and made quite a fool of himself. The night before his return by plane to Bujumbura, a big party had taken place with most of the Shell senior managers, and Paul had been quite inebriated. He overslept the next morning and missed his plane. Instead of simply rebooking his flight on the next plane the following day to Bujumbura and eating humble pie, he had impulsively chartered a small plane and flown to Bujumbura at great expense. Subsequently, he had presented the bill to the company, which had caused a major uproar, but De Freitas made him swallow the costs of his foolish decision. I was warned about these traits in his character and that he was also very much a nitpicker.

My final days in Léopoldville before leaving for Burundi and my next adventure were packed with the now well-known farewell parties. Also, these were my final days with Gilberte, who seemed upset, as our relationship was so unexpectedly terminated by my transfer. We certainly made the best of our final days, and she assured me that she would be awaiting my return with great anticipation. Little did I know at that time that bets were being laid on the first guy who would conquer her romantic attentions following my departure. The vultures in the expat community were swirling around her already.

Meanwhile, I was trying to get some information about Burundi and Rwanda, not an easy task, but I managed to at least find out bits and pieces about the history of both countries, which I could extract from a few local expats. The parties continued until Gilberte and I had one more evening together on the town, with another dinner in the Belgian Steak House and a round of dancing and boozing at the nightclub. That night would be our last one together.

19

Arrival in Burundi

Through Shell's travel agent, I planned to leave on November 19, 1964, on the direct flight to Bujumbura from N'djili Airport, a flight of nearly four hours. Despite all the political troubles and military action, the commercial flights were still operating normally, and a very uneventful flight brought me to my next place of residence for the following nearly five months. The flight allowed me to spend time rummaging through my notes, assembled from my discussions prior to my departure with colleagues and acquaintances in the expat community regarding the history and situation in Rwanda and Burundi.

Four centuries ago, a tribe of cattle owners had moved from Ethiopia to the lush shores of Lake Tanganyika. This was the Watutsi tribe, or Tutsi—shrewd, proud, cruel, very tall, and striking people. Together with their impressive lyre-horned cattle, they so overwhelmed the already established tribe in the area, the Bahutus, or Hutus—tiny people, patient, hardworking and irascible—that they enslaved them, and the Hutus became the serfs of the Royal Tutsis, although they made up 86 percent of the population.

During the colonial days from 1885 to 1962, Ruanda-Urundi was first colonized by the Germans and later the Belgians. After World War I, the serf-master relationship between the tribes was maintained, although Ruanda-Urundi was a Belgian colony. In 1959, the Hutus in Ruanda drove one hundred thousand Tutsis out of Rwanda, including their king, the mwami. When independence was declared in 1962, both countries' names were changed, and the Hutus were the reigning tribe in what is now Rwanda, while the Tutsis ruled a monarchy in the newly named country, Burundi. Hutus and Tutsis continued fighting on and off, culminating in a real slaughter in 1963, when an estimated fifty thousand Tutsis were killed in Rwanda. This genocide resulted in a major exodus of Tutsis to neighboring countries, such as Uganda, Burundi, and the eastern Congo.

Though still a Belgian colony in 1959, Mwami Mwambutsa IV, the Tutsi king of Urundi, requested the Belgians separate Ruanda and Urundi. This was granted, and the new country, Burundi, was governed under Belgian tutelage by Prince Louis Rwagasore, who was assassinated in 1961 with the colonial authorities apparently very much involved, as they feared that their commercial interests in Burundi would be hurt by Rwagasore.

The country had been encumbered by fighting between the tribes, with the minority Tutsi dominating as they had in Rwanda, massacring Hutus by the thousands and increasing tensions leading to the independence of the country on July 1, 1962.

Mwami Mwambutsa IV became king of the newly independent country and appointed André Muhirwa, a Tutsi, as prime minister.[14]

Burundi is a landlocked country in the Great Lakes region of Eastern Africa bordered by Rwanda to the north, Tanganyika to the east and south, and the Republic of Congo to the west. The official languages in Burundi are Kirundi and French. The capital of Burundi is Bujumbura, renamed after independence from the former Usumbura. This town has a total population of around seventy thousand and is located on the very northeastern shore of Lake Tanganyika. Through the harbor, coffee, hides, tin concentrates, and cotton are shipped by barge to Kigoma in Tanganyika. Petroleum products are also shipped from Mombasa, Kenya, by the East African Railways to Kigoma and, again, by barge to Bujumbura.

Since I was arriving in November, it would be the beginning of the wet season, which starts in October and usually ends toward the beginning of May. Days would be clear with clouds building up toward the middle of the day, resulting in torrential rains lasting at most a few hours to leave way again for clear skies in the mid to late afternoon. Temperatures would be reasonably constant during the day at about thirty degrees Celsius and around seventeen to eighteen degrees at night. The temperatures are quite comfortable despite the tropical climate because of the higher altitude of Bujumbura, at about 775 meters.

Having done my homework, at least I had some idea of the basic political, geographic, and statistical background of

---

[14]   http://en.wikipedia.org/wiki/History_of_Burundi.

Rwanda, Burundi, and the town of Bujumbura. Otherwise, I had no idea what to expect. I did not even know what Paul Bröcker looked like, as they did not have any photograph of him in Leo's HR office.

I arrived and cleared rapidly through immigration and customs, and since the first European I noted past the gate addressed me by name, I had located Paul without a hitch. He seemed a clean-cut individual, slender and a bit underweight. Paul took me through the rather spacious airport, and outside his Peugeot 403, a solid beige, four-door vehicle, was waiting for us with a driver dressed in a safari suit with a Shell badge above his left suit pocket. I was introduced to Oscar, who was a Congolese, as Paul told me on the way to town. Oscar would be with me for my entire stay. We would have many experiences together, and he proved to be a loyal and dependable chap with excellent driving skills. I must say, the unexpected luxury of a personal driver hit me only sometime later.

Paul had arranged for me to spend the first two weeks of my stay at one of the local hotels. The Palace Hotel was inaptly named. It was certainly a hotel, but the comparison with a palace was far from reality. I put my suitcase in my room and rejoined Paul in the lobby. We immediately drove to the Shell office in the main part of town. Paul introduced me to the staff, and a special introduction was made to Mrs. Katharina Loval, an attractive middle-aged European lady, who was the secretary to the regional manager Rwanda/Burundi. I would inherit this lofty title from Paul for the duration of his absence on home leave.

Mrs. Loval, who was of White Russian extraction and married to a Belgian working for a Belgian company in

Bujumbura, would prove to be invaluable, especially during my first weeks after Paul's departure, as she knew where all the documents were hidden and which one would be relevant for certain situations. I could not have been luckier to have her on my side.

20

Avenue du Ravin 12 and Handover-Takeover of Shell Region Burundi-Rwanda

Avenue du Ravin12

Following our review of the program, Paul handed me a sheaf of additional papers, which he thought I might like

to review that evening in preparation for our first major review the next day. He also invited me to his home, which, as it turned out, would be my home during the period of his absence. Shell had rented this bungalow for the regional manager, so in that capacity, I would be the tenant at "12 Rue du Ravin." I packed my homework, and Paul drove us to his, our, home in the Peugeot, since Oscar was no longer on duty for the evening.

We drove toward the outskirts of town into a hilly section of Bujumbura where the more well-to-do citizens and most of the expats were living. The area was lush with palm trees and other typical tropical vegetation. It struck me how well the homes and gardens seemed to be maintained, with bougainvillea, the predominant flowers, in every garden, together with palm and banana trees, birds of paradise, and a variety of other tropical plants. We arrived at the Shell rented residence and approached a big gate. A gardener, who also came with the house, appeared from nowhere to open it. We drove about a hundred meters; the driveway swerved around a white, very attractive bungalow, enveloped with flowering bougainvillea and surrounded by a large lawn and lots of borders planted with the earlier mentioned variety of tropical trees, as well as flamboyant acacia, jacaranda, and frangipani. It seemed like a small oasis away from town. We drove under a covered part of the driveway, which passed under an arch connecting the bedrooms and the living quarters, rejoining the entry driveway again.

Paul and I alighted from the car to meet with Monique, Paul's Dutch wife, who welcomed me at the front door. She seemed a very warm person who did not waste time to express her concern that Paul had taken me to the office first after my long flight and not given me a break and a rest at the hotel. Immediately, I took a liking to her and said that I appreciated her husband's efforts to get me properly briefed as quickly as possible. In addition, I thought that the sooner I was ready, the more relaxed he would be, knowing that the company would be in good hands during their absence on home leave.

Following a pleasant evening with Paul and Monique, Paul took me back to the Palace Hotel well before midnight. Although I wanted to collapse into my bed, I noticed an invasion of cockroaches in the room. I battled the horrors for a while, but they were too well ensconced in and around the heavy window draperies, probably a leftover from the colonial days! I was too tired to be bothered to fight the buggers any longer. The next day, I made sure to ask the front desk to give the room a thorough going-over and to make sure that the roaches at least would be minimized.

"Day one" in the office was very productive, and we covered the program points very thoroughly. I was also introduced to our Burundi representative, a tall and lanky Tutsi, who was basically our liaison with the owners of the Shell service stations and with Hatton and Cookson, a subsidiary of Unilever, our sales agents in Burundi, as well as in Rwanda. As I had learned, we did not own the gasoline stations, but we had contractual arrangements with the owners to deliver the gasoline, diesel, and other products. We would offer them financing, if required, and we installed Shell-owned pumps and tanks. We did not impose sales quotas, but we did expect them to work with us on a budgeted quantity of product throughput. Hatton and Cookson were responsible for the delivery of any of our products that the stations ordered from them directly to be delivered from the various Shell depots in Bujumbura.

That evening, we dined with Monique in a surprisingly good local restaurant not far from the office. I liked the intimacy of this small, airy restaurant with its large outdoor seating and view of the street, where a constant buzz enlivened the scene. I would return here often during my stay. During dinner, Monique asked how I was faring in the Hotel Palace and I could not resist telling my cockroaches story. Monique turned to her husband and asked him pointblank why he had put me in this hotel. Paul said that he did not think another accommodation would have been appropriate, short of offering the guestroom in their home. Immediately following this comment, Monique said with a raised voice: "But Paul, Hans would have been more than welcome to stay with us; he would have gotten used to the house, and it would be fun to have a guest like him in our home!" I was not quite sure how to react, and mumbled that I was quite happy with the arrangements and that I certainly did not want to impose on their privacy. Monique did not want to hear any of my mild protestations and told Paul that she expected me to be their guest as of the next day. So, it was, and after another successful day covering our daily program, I moved into the guest room at "Rue du Ravin." I would stay there until my departure the following April for Léo. So, until Paul and Monique's departure on home leave, we were a happy threesome, although I never thought Paul was quite comfortable with this arrangement.

Paul and I would come home from work on the remaining days before our trip to Rwanda, and we would enjoy our lunches and dinner in the spacious dining room, but not before we would have taken a beer to the covered veranda connected to the living room. This veranda was completely open from floor to ceiling and was protected by a fancy iron grille with anti-mosquito screening stretched behind it. Outside, a banana tree was rustling against the grille and showed a new bundle of bananas growing in its top. A wealth of tropical flowers was also very visible, and beyond one could see the garden, a lush lawn bordered by more flowers and tropical vegetation.

As I had arrived in November, I experienced the start of the rainy season in Burundi, which had two different periods. From November until February, primarily short rains fall. Then the long rains begin and continue until about late May. These rainfalls would be torrential at times, preceded by a buildup of dark, gloomy towers of clouds, but lasting no more than an hour or two at most. The buildup would usually start in the middle of the day, and around lunchtime, the heavens would unload. However, the veranda was a good place to sit even during the rains, as it was completely sheltered.

What a great place to relax, linger, and enjoy a good Primus beer, while watching the torrents of water splash against the vegetation just outside the veranda. Paul was always keen to have his beer and put a few away without any pain. He became more relaxed and talkative after a few. He would tell me more about the politics in Burundi, and the current horrible developments in the Congo. He seemed far better informed than most of us in Léopoldville, mainly because of his close connections with the embassies in town. Monique was also quite a storyteller and would not hesitate to relate some local gossip about the comings and goings at the embassies and the expats' way of life in town. Paul explained that he had a very close relationship with the British Embassy, as Shell was 40 percent owned by British shareholders, the remaining 60 percent owned by the Dutch.

Since there was no Dutch Embassy in either Rwanda or Burundi, the British Embassy and its ambassador were therefore our logical and primary diplomatic connection. Paul would meet with regularity with Ambassador John Bennett, the current British envoy, to exchange political information, as well as anything happening with the oil industry. He said he would introduce me to Bennett in the next few days, as well as to his very helpful secretary, who we could rely on for support to arrange for the necessary Burundi government connections. Paul mentioned that he would also introduce me to the American military attaché at the US Embassy in Kigali. He had developed a very close relationship with Lieutenant-Colonel Fred Wagoner and stayed with him and his wife Jane during overnight visits to Kigali. I was certainly looking forward to meeting all the brass, with whom I had not anticipated working so closely during my stay in Burundi and Rwanda. Our connections with the United States ambassador were limited more to a social level. However, as Paul explained, because of our close contact with Ambassador Bennett, he did not see a specific need to cozy up to too many other diplomats.

Paul and I worked hard on the program and made good progress. Importantly, our visits to the depots gave me good insight into the location and importance of our supplies. Particularly interesting was the location of our aviation gasoline, large lubricants, and LPG canisters. The latter came in twenty- and one-hundred-pound sizes, as was the case with all our products.

These and our other lubricants, as well as drums of aviation gasoline, were shipped by Shell Tanganyika, through Dar-es-Salaam, or by Kenya Shell through the port of Mombasa. They would travel to Kigoma on Lake Tanganyika with the former and famous Tanganyika Railways, now called the East African Railways and Harbours Corporation, and from there were transported by barge to the harbor of Bujumbura. We visited the Socopétrol tanks in the harbor district. Paul explained that we had accumulated a large supply of gasoline because of over-stockage, to be prepared for the rising level of Lake Tanganyika, which would prevent the barges from loading at Kigoma and unloading in Bujumbura. When the lake's rising waters steadied, it offered us an advantage for transshipping excess stocks to our colleague in Goma, eastern Congo.

The eastern Congo could not be supplied at this stage from Kampala, Uganda, because of the closing of the border between Uganda and the Congo, due to the political situation between the two countries. I was fascinated about all these intrigues and problems that we were having in this small Shell company, and I realized that with Paul's imminent departure, all problems would be mine!

On November 25, Paul received an urgent call from Ambassador Bennett. Apparently, a major military operation had taken place the previous day, November 24, in Stanleyville. Belgian paratroopers had been dropped on the airport by American Air Force planes, and they subsequently liberated the roughly three thousand whites after moving on to Stanleyville.[15] These whites were the ones who had been held hostage by Gbenye, the communist rebel leader, and our colleague André Desmaret was among them. Apparently two dozen had been killed, including the so-called American spy, the Reverend Dr. Paul Carlsson. Many were also wounded, but there was no news about André.

The ambassador promised to keep us posted on any additional developments and asked us to do likewise in case we learned more from Shell Léopoldville. Immediately, Paul sent a telex to De Freitas, asking him to let us have more details and especially news about André's well-being. As usual, a reply would take a day, if not two, to reach us. Communications, as Paul explained to me, were rather dismal, to say the least. Telex was the primary mode of communication throughout the area, but it functioned very slowly. Telephone communication was virtually impossible with Léo, although it was working quite well in town. Letters to head office took about four days, with a return reply of about the same amount of time. I would experience this lack of communication during my three months as the regional manager. As I learned, it became crucial to make one's decisions first, and inform one's superior of actions taken afterward and just hope for the best. For sure, that became my destiny.

Meanwhile, Paul took advantage of the call from Ambassador Bennett to set up an appointment with him that afternoon, prior to our departure on the next day for our visit to Rwanda. The visit turned out to be very cordial.

---

15   *Dragon Rouge: The Rescue of Hostages in the Congo*, by Fred E. Wagoner.

In addition, I met the ambassador's secretary, Janet Brewster, a middle-aged lady, who clearly was well in charge of the administrative office of her boss.

John Bennett was not high on formalities, and we immediately were on a first-name basis. We discussed the general background of my stay in Bujumbura, and he urged me to not hesitate to seek his advice and information. Of course, he also would appreciate my briefing him on any important developments in the petroleum industry. John proceeded to tell us that the Chinese influence through the prime minister, Alban Niamoya, and other government officials was steadily increasing and had caused a lot of concern about the future stability of the country.

Mwami Mwambutsa IV, the king of Burundi, had been keeping his distance from the Chinese, even refusing to accept the formal credentials of the Chinese ambassador. It was rumored that the Chinese were using Burundi as a staging ground for further subversive activities in the Congo. Earlier in the year, a defector from the Chinese embassy, an interpreter, had stated that Mao had said: "Burundi is the way to the Congo, and when the Congo falls, the whole of Africa will follow."[16]

We left the embassy on that final note. I was happy to have met this excellent representative of Her Majesty the Queen. We would be meeting many times again and experience some interesting times together.

Meanwhile, our "handover-takeover" program had proceeded well. I had met most of those who would be

---

[16]   F. R. Metrowich, *Africa and Communism*, Chapter 6, "Our Men from Havana," page 143.

working with me professionally. I was especially taken by our Italian transporter, Grassetto. Shell leased trucks from him, and his company made our deliveries of lubricants, drums of aviation gasoline, and our LPG canisters. Grassetto would prove to be most helpful to me. I also met with most of our *confrères*—the managers of Mobil Oil, Texaco, Pétrocongo, and British Petroleum; I would have regular contact with them in the months to come.

On February 11 that year, a major currency devaluation had taken place in Burundi. Thus, our treasury resources had been limited to those available on the day of the devaluation, approximately two million Burundi francs, which was not enough to operate. Finance/Léo had been asked to provide us with the necessary documentation to ask for an exemption of the currency availability ruling. Paul was quite well informed about the competitors' financial positions as well, which might give us an edge in the marketplace.

Saturday's mail brought a rather surprising letter for me personally from Edmond Becker, the sales manager of Shell Léopoldville. He was reflecting on my interim appointment in Bujumbura and the experience this would provide to enhance my career. He continued to say, and I quote in French: "*Les rapports verbaux qui me sont parvenus a votre sujet, ne sont pas particulièrement favorables.*" ("The verbal reports I have received about you have not been particularly favorable") I was rather taken aback by this comment, and could not quite figure out why Becker was aiming his displeasure at me in this very direct way. Perhaps it was a way to get back at me for my inappropriately inviting De Freitas to my birthday party and not him and his wife.

I put the grim thoughts aside and decided to treat his comments as a positive push toward my future performance in my position in Bujumbura. After all, Shell would benefit from my positive performance, particularly during these stressful days the region was experiencing.

I decide to write him back, and did so during the weekend, saying: "Your comments concerning my earlier performance during my first months in Léopoldville have been like a 'whip lash' to inspire me to put a very strong effort into my job and attitude during the next several months as Interim-Regional Director in Bujumbura. I have already been inspired by the briefings of our colleague Paul Bröcker during my first ten days in Bujumbura and I assure you that you will not be disappointed in my ultimate performance on the job."

I did not hear again from Becker, and I concluded that he must have decided to let time take its course and that the way I would conduct myself during my assignment would have to speak for itself. That very day, we also received a telex reply from De Freitas. André Desmaret had been found alive on the square where the Stanley monument stood. When the rebels started firing indiscriminately into the group of white hostages, apparently, he had could dive behind a concrete bench, which saved his life.

De Freitas confirmed that some thirty whites had been killed, and many were wounded. Desmaret was in shock and had to be repatriated to Belgium to be treated for mental distress. De Freitas would be sending more details to us by mail. Paul confirmed the message with Ambassador Bennett, and we discussed the event among ourselves, hoping that

André would not have any permanent psychological distress from his ordeal.

We did reflect on the situation, as one could never be sure in this very volatile part of Africa what would happen next. We could only hope that we would be spared any of the violence André had just experienced.

21

First Visit to Rwanda

**Paul Bröcker - Baganzicaha –
Oscar, our Congolese driver**

Finally, on Monday, November 30, Paul and I were ready to make our trip to Rwanda. I was excited to start the journey, as it would be my first trip into the countryside of either Burundi or Rwanda. I knew we would be traveling through hilly country with small villages scattered along the road. As we traveled north to the Rwanda border, we would visit a client in the small village of Kayanza and continue to Kigali, the capital of Rwanda, by way of Butare, to meet with other clients. In Kigali, I would meet our Rwanda Shell representative, Baganzicaha.

The trip was about 110 miles, 175 kilometers, on a winding road going up and down the hills and through forested country. We would see some coffee plantations, still the main cash crop of Burundi. As Paul had already mentioned, the roads were made of packed dirt and could be very slippery right after a rainfall.

Rwanda was slightly less than two-thirds the size of the Netherlands, with a population of about three million. It bordered Burundi, once part of Rwanda-Urundi, to the north; Lake Kivu and the Congo were on the west; Uganda was to the north, and, finally, Tanganyika was to the east.

We were sitting in the back of our Peugeot, Oscar driving like the old pro he was, while Paul took time to tell me more about Rwanda. As I had learned already, Tutsi and Hutus had settled in the area four centuries ago, but eventually there was increasing strife between the tribes. The political situation had been very unstable, because of the tribal system maintained by the Belgians after World War I, where the Tutsi were favored and allowed to rule the country. Following a rumored assassination attempt on Kayibanda, the leader of a Hutu political party, the Hutus slaughtered some one hundred thousand Tutsis, and some 150,000 fled to the bordering countries. It was not until

1961 that a referendum was held, leading to the creation of a new republic dominated by the Hutus. This ended the reign of the mwamis as kings in Rwanda.

The then-reigning king left the country, and Kayibanda was named the first prime minister of the new republic. This would not end the political and tribal strife in the country, and incursions of the exiled Tutsi into Rwanda killed thousands more between 1961 and 1962.

By UN mandate, Rwanda and Urundi both became independent countries in 1962, when Urundi was renamed Burundi. Following an election, Kayibanda became the first elected president of Rwanda.[17]

Against the background of tribal unrest, the last few months had been rather quiet, but travel between Burundi and Rwanda required special permits from both government authorities to cross the borders. Paul showed me the special pass needed to go through customs in Burundi, as well as in Rwanda. In addition, we were issued passes to enable us to cross the military border control points. Paul had ample experience with these crossings, as he traveled regularly to Kigali by car. However, this trip we would experience an unexpected turn of events. We were chatting away and talking about the terrible tribal clashes and death tolls resulting from the many Tutsi incursions into Rwanda and the horrible developments in Stanleyville, as well as in other areas of the Congo because of the rebel activities, when Paul suddenly sat upright as a large truck with a Shell emblem passed us on the road. The truck was loaded with drums and was heading in the opposite direction from where

---

[17]   http://en.wikipedia.org/wiki/History_of_Rwanda.

we had just come. Immediately, Paul told Oscar to turn around, follow the truck, pass him, and make him stop on the narrow road.

Paul jumped out of our car and ran to the truck and, after identifying himself as the Shell regional manager, asked the driver where he was going. The driver clearly did not understand all the commotion, but he complied with Paul's request and showed his delivery and transit papers. Paul looked at them and, having already seen that the drums on the truck contained aviation gasoline, or "avgas," he exclaimed, "Hans this is the load of avgas that I have been waiting for to be delivered in Kigali!"

I knew what he was talking about, as the delay in delivery of the avgas from Mombasa through Kampala and finally to Kigali had put our relationship with two of our main customers in difficulty; they both risked being grounded for lack of fuel. A recent closing of the border with the Congo and Uganda had further complicated the situation. Paul showed me the papers he had just scrutinized and pointed to the error. The destination of the drums had been indicated as Bujumbura, Kigali, not Kigali, Rwanda, so both the customs and police on either side of the border had allowed the truck to be cleared, and hence the driver was on his way to Bujumbura.

Paul explained patiently to the driver what had gone wrong and pointed to the error in the destination of the payload on the truck. The driver seemed panicked, but Paul told him to relax, and explained that he, as the Shell regional manager, would make sure that everything would be straightened out. He told the driver to turn the truck around, not an easy task on the narrow road, but somehow, on an even narrower path, the truck driver managed to make the U-turn and followed us to the border. After a solid half-hour drive, we arrived at the first border police post.

Paul alighted from our car and walked to the post. He was confronted by an impressive-looking army officer, who asked, with an air of great authority, why this truck was heading toward the border again, after it had just been cleared for Bujumbura. Paul explained patiently what had gone wrong and that the truck should have been going to Kigali and not to Bujumbura. The lieutenant indicated that it would be nearly impossible to reverse the authority for the truck, as clearance had been given and could not be reversed.

Paul mentioned to him that the arrival of the truck in Bujumbura would create a real problem, as the Treasury had not cleared any foreign reserves to import this big of a load of aviation gasoline. He suggested that it would be a lot easier if a document would be created to allow the return of the truck to Rwanda, as this would certainly avoid the problem of punishing those responsible for authorizing clearance for the truck to enter the country.

The lieutenant seemed unconvinced, but the inherent threat Paul had outlined for sanctions against those who inappropriately imported the avgas made him think. It took a few minutes and further discussions in Kirundi, which we could not follow, when the lieutenant said that he could not sign any papers, nor could he make the decision to allow the truck to proceed back to Rwanda. However, he would take Paul to meet with the captain and commander of the post personally, and they would have to drive up into the hills to do this. Meanwhile, he said, the truck and the driver would stay under guard, and to assure that we would not do anything untoward, like driving off and circumventing the orders to stay put, he pointed to me and said, "That gentleman is now arrested and will stay in that hut under guard by this soldier until we return from our visit to the captain." Against Paul's mild protestations, I was marched off to a small hut on the side of the road and ordered by my guard to sit on a small crate inside. My guard stayed outside, and I could see Paul being driven off in a jeep by the lieutenant and his driver up a hill toward an unknown destination.

After a half hour, my rifle-toting guard joined me, and I took the opportunity to ask him how long it might take for Paul and the lieutenant to return. The soldier seemed friendly and not too concerned about my temporary status as a prisoner. "About two hours and a half," he said, as the drive to the location where the captain was holed up was about one hour, and he figured a discussion of at least half an hour and a return trip another hour. So much for comfort, as the heat in the hut was increasingly bothersome, as it must have also been for the soldier, who after about fifteen minutes inside seated on another crate, repaired outside to take a breather. About another half hour later, he returned. He asked if I was thirsty and if I would perhaps like a cold Primus beer. I could not believe that he would ask me this question, but he was very serious, and when I replied positively, he asked me if I had some money, so he could get us a couple of beers. I gave him a few francs, and, leaving his rifle leaning against the wall inside the hut, he disappeared. Clearly, I had no plans to use his rifle for any escape opportunity, as I felt comfortable enough with the situation and did not think that any heroic effort on my part would improve things one iota.

So, the rifle stayed where it was, and the soldier, true to his word, returned, and, yes, to my great relief, he carried a couple of nice, cold bottles of Primus. This Heineken product was a godsend, as I was about dried out due to the heat in the hut. The soldier clearly was also ready to enjoy his beverage, and together we sipped on our bottles. I treasured every drop, and we exchanged small talk about my background, nationality, and my work at Shell. I learned little about him other than that he was born in Bujumbura and had been some years in the army.

We finished our beer, and the soldier went outside again to stand guard. I reflected on this odd situation, but nothing could be done about it, other than patiently await Paul's return and hope for a release of our truck with the necessary pass to return to Rwanda. I must have dozed off when the soldier reentered suddenly to tell me that the jeep was returning and should be there at any moment. I ventured to the door and could see the jeep careening down the last stretch of the mountainside toward the hut. Paul alighted from the jeep followed by the lieutenant. Paul, a big smile on his face, waved a piece of paper, which clearly was our pass. Indeed, as he recalled, he had been in quite a discussion with the captain, who had not been very much inclined to cooperate, but Paul's threat to immediately return to Bujumbura and to alert the Treasury Department of the obstinacy of the captain in relation to the illegal importation of a large cargo of aviation gasoline, for which no foreign exchange had been requested, made the captain apparently change his mind. Finally, he had given Paul a pass instructing the army post to allow the return of the truck to Rwanda. The instructions were also given to the customs post, which also fell under his command.

"LAISSEZ-PASSER" to travel to Rwanda

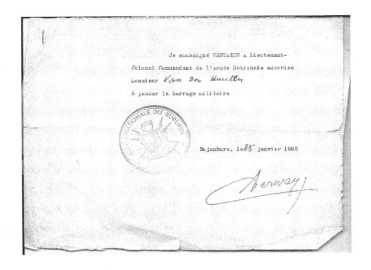

Unceremoniously, my captivity was ended, and Paul and I could leave with Oscar, the Shell truck now ambling behind us toward the customs post, where, upon reading the *Laissez-Passer*, a guard opened the barricade, and the procession of Peugeot and truck proceeded through "no-man's-land" to the Rwanda customs post. The officials there were surprised to see the Shell truck return, but after Paul explained that the dispatchers in Uganda had made a mistake and that the aviation gasoline on the truck was dearly needed in Kigali, the customs officials waved us through without even a further blink of an eye!

We had only the Rwanda Army's border post to cross, and the truck would be safely on its way to Kigali, where we knew our customers would be clamoring for the load of avgas. We approached the soldiers at the post, and they simply raised the post's bar and waved us through. We could only surmise that they did not want to be bothered with an investigation and figured that if we could pass already through three other obstacles, they would not be able to stop us from proceeding. So, onward we went, telling the truck driver where to go in Kigali and that we would make sure our representative would be there to meet him. We continued following the dirt road to Kigali, passing several small villages while driving through undulating hills thickly grown with tropical trees and shrubs. The weather was very pleasant considering the tropical climate; the rains had not bothered us on this trip, and the skies were clear, although dotted with large cloud formations.

We arrived in Kigali, and Paul told Oscar to head immediately for our small office to meet with Baganzicaha to make sure the avgas would be immediately directed to the company's bush pilots, so they would not be stranded at the airport for lack of aviation gasoline. Having taken care of this essential business, Paul introduced me properly to Baganzicaha, a graying Tutsi in his midfifties. He seemed a very deliberate yet gentle person, and I knew from Paul's earlier description of him that we could count on him to execute our business requirements. But, according to Paul, we needed to keep a tight leash on him to make sure things were done in a timely fashion, as time for Africans was not always in step with European time.

We set out our plans for our visit, which Paul had already outlined in an earlier telex, and asked whether the meetings with Hatton and Cookson—a company that acted as our sales agent for Ruanda and Burundi, as well as the banks and other Kigali clients—were confirmed. Baganzicaha assured us that this was the case and handed us the schedule for the next day's visits. He also confirmed that I would be staying in one of the guesthouses of Unilever, as Paul had suggested. Dinner was also planned that evening with the American military attaché, Lieutenant Colonel Fred Wagoner, and his wife, Jane. So, it seemed that our schedule was well in place, and we proceeded to the Unilever guesthouse to put my suitcase in my room.

The guesthouse was in a lot containing several one-story office buildings; it was a rather dusty-looking place with a sprinkling of palm trees and low shrubs, but lacking any charm or attractiveness. In any event, as Paul told me, there were no hotels in Kigali suitable for Western travelers, and this was one of the few places available to business contacts of Hatton and Cookson. The dusty lot resembled most of what I had seen so far of the town of Kigali. We had driven on the only stretch of paved road, which extended for less than five hundred meters through the center of town. The rest was packed dirt with buildings and shops on each side of the main road, as well as other streets in the center of town. Kigali was considerably smaller than Bujumbura, and lacked any appeal.

Paul took me to the only part of town that seemed to have several nicer homes, clearly the area where government officials lived, as well as embassy staff and the expat community and local senior businessmen. We arrived at a rather nice-looking home, which was the residence of the Wagoners. Fred opened the door and welcomed us inside into a very spacious, nicely decorated living room. It had an adjoining veranda that gave a view on a small but well-kept garden with a lawn surrounded by an array of tropical trees, plants, and flowers, as well as the ubiquitous bougainvillea. We were seated, and Jane joined us. I immediately took a liking to both Fred and Jane, as they were a very warm and outgoing couple. Indeed, their American heritage could not be denied, yet they both had been abroad long enough to have a more international social approach.

We had a cozy dinner, which gave us a chance, in addition to enjoying an excellent meal, to explain my mission for the next several months while Paul and Monique were on home leave.

After dinner, we enjoyed coffee and cognac, and then Paul drove me back to the guest house and returned to the Wagoners' residence, where he routinely spent the night when visiting Kigali.

The next day, we visited Hatton and Cookson, which, as our sales agents, would have to be consulted about all issues concerning Shell in Rwanda. Mr. Nubourg, regional director, was an easy-going fellow, who introduced me to his assistant in charge of all Shell matters within Hatton and Cookson. We discussed the local market requirements, and it became clear how dependent Shell, as well as all the other oil companies were on timely deliveries from Kampala. Shell was the only company with any storage capacity of gasoline, but a subterranean tank of ten thousand gallons was all that was available for the country. We discussed the capital budget for Rwanda, which I had already reviewed with Paul prior to our arrival. The visit of our technical supervisor from Léo in the beginning of the year also was reviewed. Finally, we discussed at length the increasing tensions caused by the turmoil in the Congo. The situation with the border closing between Uganda and Congo was already a considerable burden on all the oil companies, as their operations in eastern Congo were now supplied with special transit permits from the Rwanda government, and trucks were passing through the borders of Rwanda and traveling onward to Goma.

We urged Mr. Nubourg to make sure to keep us fully posted if there were any developments in this area, so, if necessary, we could take measures to secure an ongoing supply to Goma. We spent the rest of the afternoon with visits to our banks and a few important clients in Kigali.

It had been a full day, which we happily ended with cocktails and dinner, again at the home of Colonel Wagoner, by now Fred, and his wife, Jane. Kigali was not endowed with any good restaurants, so the hospitality of the Wagoners was a true blessing. Paul drove me again to the unglamorous lodging facilities of Unilever, and I retreated for the night to be ready for the continuation of our trip the next day toward Gisenyi and Goma.

22

Gisenyi, Goma, and Lake Kivu

Paul came to fetch me early, as the trip to Gisenyi and Goma would take about three hours to cover the 150 kilometers, or seventy-five miles, again on an unpaved road, dry and dusty. Yet our Oscar was driving as if it was a beautifully tarred road. It was amazing how he controlled his speed and side slipped through some of the more challenging curves. After a while, I became quite relaxed with the way he was driving. On we went, and at Ruhengeri, we turned left on the road continuing to Gisenyi. It would be some months before I would be back on this road, but for a totally different reason.

Arriving at Gisenyi, Paul suggested that we first visit Goma, a twin city to Gisenyi, but across the border in the Congo. The border crossing did not give us any problems; we just showed our Dutch passports, and we were waved on. Paul wanted me to meet Ivan de Stoop, our colleague and regional manager for the eastern Congo. Ivan was a bachelor and quite an entrepreneurial type, as I would find out during the next few months. As we would spend the night in Gisenyi in a local hotel and move on the next day back to Bujumbura, which would be a trip of about five to six hours covering some 350 kilometers, or 220 miles, Ivan invited us for dinner. However, we first returned to Gisenyi to visit our largest customer in Rwanda, Brasseries et Limonadéries du Rwanda, better known as Bralirwa.[18]

The Dutch brewer Heineken had a partial ownership of this company and provided the technical staff. We met with the manager of the brewery and a few of his marketing staff. They explained that the parent company in Léopoldville started the brewery in 1959 to provide beer directly to the eastern markets of the Congo and Rwanda. The location was chosen because of its strategic position on Lake Kivu, close to the airport of Goma, with good road connections, although dirt ones, to the main towns and markets. Beer could also be shipped to Bukavu at the southern end of the lake. As Rudolf Bak had already explained to me during my first days in Léo, the lake also contains methane gas, which could be extracted and provide an additional energy source. However, they also needed our gasoline and diesel fuel, as well as lubricants and LPG canisters. Since Hatton and Cookson provided the sales support for Shell, Paul did not have frequent contact with the managers at Bralirwa. But since this was one of our largest customers, he wanted them to know that he was leaving for three months and that I was his replacement during this time.

Just in case a major problem arose, they also knew that they could communicate with Ivan de Stoop, who would be instantly connected to the Hatton and Cookson's office in Gisenyi to sort out any issues and keep us informed by

---

[18]   http://www.bralirwa.com.

telex in Bujumbura for additional support if needed. We visited the brewery, which was a very modern installation amid impoverished townships and countryside homesteads.

After a few hours at the brewery, concluded by a sampling of their Primus beer, Paul and I returned to Goma. I was impressed again by the wide boulevards lined with palm trees and white and pink hibiscus. It was a sharp contrast with the undoubtedly once grand homes—now shabby— lining the boulevard on the mountainside of the town facing the lake. However, the conflicts had also affected Goma, and many of its well-to-do Belgian inhabitants had fled for better times in Belgium. Yet we got an excellent impression of the lovely setting, which was still there to be admired.

Goma and Gisenyi are on the western branch of the Great Rift Valley in Kivu Province, and some fifteen kilometers, or eleven miles, due south of the crater of the active Nyiragongo Volcano.

I wished we had more time to do some tourist sightseeing, especially in the Albert National Park, well-known for its gorillas. I never got to visit this great natural resource and its animals during my time in this part of Africa. During dinner, Ivan explained that due to the elevation of the lake, at fifteen hundred meters, or forty-five hundred feet, the dreaded bilharzia disease, which is transmitted through worms to humans, is not present in the lake. He also confirmed Rudolf Bak's story about the methane gas in the lake and the inherent danger of an explosion. Nevertheless, the gas is also taken from the lake and can be used for industrial purposes, although this was an underused resource now.

I enjoyed meeting Ivan, and he assured me that we would be in close touch during my time in Bujumbura, and if he could be of any assistance, I would just have to let him know. Little did we know at that time how much we would get involved on two wholly different issues, but I knew that I would enjoy my collaboration with this spunky Belgian.

We spent the night in a nondescript hotel, and the next morning we left for Bujumbura by way of Gitarama, where we rejoined the road to Butare and onward to the border with Burundi, crossing the army and custom posts again, this time unburdened by our truck. The border guards on the Burundi side were not the same ones who were in charge when we crossed with our Shell truck. They let us through without any difficulty, proving that our passes were valid and properly stamped in Bujumbura.

Arriving at the Avenue du Ravin home, we were ready for a good shower, a Primus beer, and a good night's rest after yet another excellent meal prepared by Monique Bröcker. It had been an interesting trip and provided me with a lot for background for the months to come.

23

Ivan de Stoop and Two Other Belgians Taken Prisoner by Uganda Rifles

When we returned the next day to the office, our secretary excitedly entered Paul's office with a telex in her hand. "Read this quickly," she said. "This is very serious and urgent!" Paul read the telex and handed it to me. I quickly read the contents, and, turning to Paul, I said, "Now Ivan is truly in trouble!" The telex coming from Léopoldville told us that Ivan de Stoop and two other Belgians had been taken prisoner by the Uganda Rifles, a crack division of the Ugandan Army. Apparently, they had been captured when they entered the no-man's-zone between the border of Uganda and the Congo.

The message noted that Shell in London had been informed and had advised us to seek clarification though our connections in Africa. We immediately contacted Ambassador Bennett by phone and asked him to inquire if the British Embassy in Kampala had any more information. As our instructions were very clear not to communicate directly with our sister Shell companies, we sent a telex to

Léo suggesting that they ask Shell in Kampala for the same information. We were sure that by now the Shell network would already be activated to do the same as we proposed, but never mind an additional probe in that direction.

In addition, Paul sent a telex to Fred Wagoner apprising him of the situation and requesting any information about Ivan's imprisonment. We did not have to contact Ivan's office, as the telex had indicated that they were already in contact with Goma, as well as with the parent companies of the two Belgians involved in this situation. We had done what we could and could only speculate upon what might have possibly gone wrong with Ivan and his compatriots. Why were they at the border in the first place, and why would the Ugandan Rifles retain three Belgians in custody?

The next day, our telex worked overtime! Messages arrived from Kampala Shell via our colleagues in Léo indicating that all they knew was that Ivan had been detained with the two other Belgians because they were suspected of being spies. For which party, they could have been spying was not made clear, but the charges were apparently very serious, and we had to await further information. Shell London approached us also directly, copying De Freitas in Léo, requesting us to send them anything we could uncover about the situation. Meanwhile, Ambassador Bennett was on the phone and confirmed his discussion also by telex, which duplicated the information we had already received from Shell Uganda.

Once again, we sent another message to Fred Wagoner in Kigali, who finally came back with an equally distressing report that fully confirmed what we already knew. So, all we could do at this point was to hope that the diplomatic connections of Shell in London, as well as their contacts with the Belgian government, could put something in motion to clarify the situation and pressure the Ugandan government and army for the release of the three held in custody. We had seen Ivan only a few days before in Goma. He must have been going on his mission to the border for an unknown reason shortly after seeing us, but all we could do at this point was guess and wish for the best.

We were not in any position, as a small cog in the wheel, to assist further in a meaningful way. All we could do was to wait for information and use all our energy to make sure we would not fall behind in our work to hand over the region to me.

24

Final Days with Paul Bröcker

Paul and Monique were planning to leave on their three-month home leave on Saturday, December 12, which would give us a few more days to review our "handover-takeover" schedule and to fill in any gaps and questions that might have arisen during the past weeks. We also made a quick trip to Kitega, where we would visit a few clients. The town was the original capital of Burundi, and the base of the Archdiocese of Kitega, which was established in 1912, and the Burundi National Museum. Paul pointed out that the annual sorghum festival, *Umuganuro*,[19] would take place in the early months of next year, close to Kitega at Gishora Hill. It would be an occasion for a magnificent display of traditional dances by the court dancers, or *Intore*, and Mwami Mwambutsa IV would preside over the celebration. Paul further mentioned that the *karyenda*, a traditional African drum, used extensively at the ceremony, was the

---

[19] http://music.africamuseum.be/instruments/english/burundi/ burundi.html.

main symbol of Burundi, and that the mwami had a semi-divine status. The mwami was said to interpret the beatings of the *karyenda* into rules for the kingdom. Following independence, the national flag of Burundi was designed with a shoot of sorghum with a *karyenda* on its top in the middle of the flag, underscoring the importance of the royal drum.

We visited the archdiocese in Kitega to introduce me as the interim director and to make sure the priests knew that they could contact me directly for any of their requirements for paraffin wax. The archdiocese was the main producer of candles used in the various churches, and the wax was the main ingredient to produce the candles. We had a very amicable discussion with a few of the priests and used the occasion to exchange some thoughts about the current state of the church within the strained political environment.

Upon our return to Bujumbura, we repaired to the office for a few more hours to close the files concerning a few more outstanding issues. No further messages had arrived from Léo concerning Ivan de Stoop, so Paul sent another telex to see if they had anything else to report. Finally, Paul formally handed me the keys to the depots, his office, and the office safe, as well as the car. That evening, we celebrated the Bröckers' departure with another pleasant meal at, by now, my favorite downtown restaurant, and we closed the evening with a bottle of champagne in the garden room at the Avenue du Ravin bungalow.

The next day, I drove Paul and Monique to the airport; they were all chipper and ready to turn their backs on Bujumbura for a great three months of home leave. Monique was outlining their plans, and Paul was relaxing in the backseat of the car, knowing that the burdens of the office were now in my hands. I was just happy for them to be able to get a break. At the airport, I waited with them until the plane was called. I waved good-bye and saw the plane taxiing to the tarmac, making its turn onto the runway and finally taking off on the direct flight to Brussels.

They were gone, and I knew that I had no more counseling available in the office from Paul. I walked to the car and started to drive down the straight road back to Bujumbura from the airport. It was a long road, several kilometers; traffic was nearly totally absent on this Saturday.

While driving, and pondering my new situation as regional manager for two countries about the size of my home country, I suddenly was reminded of the letter from Raymond Becker: "*Les rapports verbaux qui me sont parvenus à votre sujet, ne sont pas particulièrement favorables.*" This line was now haunting me. I started to talk to myself loudly, and with great emphasis, I shouted, while banging on the steering wheel: "I will prove that I can do this job; I will do this job and do it well!"

Making this promise to myself was like a relief and an incentive, and in doing so, I addressed the criticism I had received from Becker. Indeed, I might not have been functioning at my true capacity in Léo, but then again, I did not feel that I had been given any real incentive to perform in my various functions. A total lack of guidance from my immediate superiors had not been too much of an inspiration.

Now, however, on this straight road, alone and driving toward my destination for the next three months, I knew that it was my duty to perform at top level. I made my vows loud and clear, and I knew it was now up to me to show results. Little did I know that I would be tested on all kind of levels in many different situations in the months to come.

Until now, except for the avgas and Ivan de Stoop episodes, it had been rather quiet. This would soon change. I returned to the office and asked my secretary to arrange for a gathering of all our staff in Bujumbura the next Monday in my office. I wanted to make sure that they were fully aware of the fact that Paul was no longer in charge and had gone to enjoy a well-deserved vacation. I also wanted to make sure that they knew that as of now, I had taken over the responsibility for the office with the inherent responsibility for everyone's activities working within the organization in Burundi for Shell.

That Monday, just before the arrival of the staff, my secretary came rushing into the office with another urgent telex from Léo. After ten days, Ivan had been released with the two other Belgians after being detained as prisoners at a luxury hotel in Fort Portal, north of Lake George. The telex only indicated that the Ugandan Rifles had followed orders from the army chief of staff to release the three, who were apparently on their way back to Goma. De Freitas sent an additional telex suggesting that I talk to De Stoop directly to get a full report from him about the border situation so we would be prepared for any future disturbances. He also directed me to avoid any undue risk in such situations. I noted his concern and sent a telex to Ivan asking him to be in touch with me as soon as he returned.

25

Christmas 1964

A few weeks later, I received a package from my father with the awaited clothing he had ordered for me at Wulfsen & Wulfsen in The Hague. I was delighted to have a new wardrobe. My new, white, tropical tuxedo would follow shortly as well through the services of Belex-Congo delivered to Brasseur, their agent in Bujumbura. I had no clue if I would be using this tuxedo, yet it would be good to have it, just in case. I had my "boy" make sure that the few borrowed clothes I brought from Léo, which I had been wearing since my arrival, would get a thorough cleaning and be packed away. At least with the arrival of my new clothes, the episode of the thefts in Léo had been closed, so onward with other matters.

The first week on my own I visited several our clients to make sure that all the orders were properly delivered per their requirements. This gave me an insight into the execution of our marketing arrangements by Hatton and Cookson, as well as the proper functioning of the deliveries through the local trucking companies. I had several meetings with the trucking companies' owners, and my second meeting with Mario Grassetto, one of the owners, was extremely cordial. I knew that I would be working well with this fellow and that he had his heart in the right place for our company's interests.

I also visited our depots many times. First, Paul had alerted me to the fact that the guards had a real propensity to sleep on the job if they were not irregularly visited and thus kept on their toes. One of the depots was in town and held most of the smaller-size lubricants and some smaller kerosene containers. However, safety was less a concern at this location, as the warehouse was in the middle of town and could be securely locked. We had a twenty-four-hour guard arrangement with a local security firm, and with additional regular visits of some of my staff and me, there was enough movement around the place to deter anyone from stealing our products. In addition, I made it a habit to visit my depots at least once a week on a spur-of-the-moment basis, so the guard was never sure when I would appear.

Our depot outside of town was a good fifteen minutes away on a curvy dirt road. It was surrounded by a high fence topped with barbed wire. Other than cutting through the fence, it would be a challenge to climb it to enter the depot. The open depot was stocked with drums of aviation gasoline, lubricants in drums, and our supply of fifty- and one-hundred-pound canisters of LNG.

The small ones were sold for home use, and the larger were primarily for industrial purposes. We had a small office at the gate, and the guards would be stationed there for twenty-four hours. Again, I made it a habit to also visit this depot on an irregular schedule both during the day as well as at night for the same reason that I visited the in-town depot, keeping them guessing about the time of my visit and thus enhancing the alertness of the guards.

Just before Christmas, I received a telex from Ivan telling me that he had arrived safely in Goma. He was not able to call me, as the telephone service between the eastern Congo and Burundi was a disaster. So, he said that he would send a note to De Freitas and a copy to me with the full details of his adventure. It would be a few days before the note would arrive, as he would send it by regular pouch to Bujumbura. Thus, I patiently waited for his note to reach me, but it would not be until after Christmas, at the earliest, before it reached the office.

Christmas was now a day away, and I had no idea what I would do, other than spending this day of celebration of the birth of Christ in the solitude of my lovely bungalow. I had sufficient food in the house, which I would prepare myself, as I had given the "houseboy" two days off, as was customary. Christmas Eve arrived, and I concocted a rather decent meal and retreated to my veranda. The temperature at night was quite comfortable, as the higher altitude cooled the atmosphere, and with the open veranda, a slight breeze would further cool the house as well. It was not even necessary to start the air conditioner. Not much was happening otherwise; I did not feel like reading and proceeded to open a new bottle of Scotch.

It was time for quiet contemplation, and it did not take long before I was drifting off with my thoughts, to the last few months before I joined Shell. I had graduated from the University of Lausanne with a degree equivalent to an MBA, as a *Licencé ès Sciènce Commerciale et Économique*. It had been a great nearly four years at the university. I had experienced a lot of personal things during those years, including an engagement to an American gal, Ann Wade, but this had been broken off a few months before I joined Shell. Shell had always been my company of choice. I also had a preliminary interview with Unilever, but unlike Shell, they would not guarantee an immediate overseas assignment. In addition, I was not too enamored of their line of business, and I felt that I could more readily match my background with the requirements Shell had put to me in my first interview with them a year before my graduation.

The hiring process started in February, and I was put through the hoops with interviews and a final panel interview, where I was "cross-examined" by six senior Shell officials. Many pertinent questions were put to me, and one particularly stood out: I was asked how I would react if an African would be my boss in any of my future assignments. I did not have to think about the answer at all and immediately responded, "Personally, I would not object to anyone overseeing me, if I can learn the ropes of the business from this person." I noted from the glances around the table that my answer was well-received. Following the panel interview, I met with the coordinating secretary, and I asked her when she thought I might start working for the company. She looked very surprised at me and said, "But, Mr. Van den Houten, you first must be accepted by the company and receive a firm offer!" Obviously, I was somewhat naïve, to say the least, but in my mind, there had never been a moment of doubt about my being offered the opportunity to work for Shell. Indeed, a week after the final panel meeting, I received a letter of appointment with a very good offer. Later I learned from one of the panel members, who was a reserve cavalry officer and a member of the Hussars of Boreel, the same regiment I belonged to, that my scholastic background and my command of four languages, as well as my straightforward replies to the panel members, had left no doubt that I deserved an offer of employment at Shell.

The first month at Shell was an indoctrination into the company. I was guided through some of the Shell basics before the actual initial training began. After this month, I joined a group of about thirty other new employees from various countries and with a mixture of educational backgrounds. We would all be together first for a week in The Hague, followed by a three-week course in Shell Center in London, and finish our indoctrination at the Shell Lensbury Club outside of London in Teddington. During the final week at this impressive facility—founded in 1920 by then Shell Chairman Henri Deterding, and used by Shell employees for social and sporting activities, as well as conferences and training courses—we were told our first assignments.

When I had been asked for my preference for a first assignment, I had indicated that I would like to be in a Francophone area, so I could continue to use my fluency of the French language. To my surprise, I learned that I was going to Léopoldville in the Congo, a country which I had not put high on my list. Nevertheless, the excitement of knowing my first destination was celebrated with several my colleagues.

Preparations for departure had taken another couple of weeks, but here I was in Burundi, not quite a year after I had joined Shell, and it was a night that I had always celebrated as a holiday with family and friends. I was drinking whiskey as if it was the end of the world. I had joined Shell, and I was facing a great challenge very early in my career. Many thoughts were milling through my head that Christmas Eve. The effect of the alcohol was not conducive to very rational thought, contemplating and reviewing my life story. So, Christmas Eve went with half a bottle of whiskey downed without any real aftereffects.

The next day, I decided to go to the office. Christmas Day was not exactly a day to be at work, but what else was there to do anyway? I picked up the mail at the post office box, and, to my great surprise, Ivan's note about his border experience was already there; it must have caught the last plane out of Goma for Burundi just before the holiday. I returned to the office with the usual stack of memos and notifications from Léo. As I reviewed the mail in the office, I also found a letter from my father. Before reading my father's epistle, I opened Ivan's letter and started to read his account.

26

Ivan de Stoop's Captivity in Fort Portal, Uganda

Ivan received a telephone call from a Belgian business acquaintance in Bujumbura, who told him that rumors were circulating that the border between Uganda and the eastern Congo might be reopened. Due to tension between the Ugandan government and the Kasavubu government in the Congo, the border had been closed for all human and commercial traffic.

Thus, supplies for Shell had been routed through Rwanda and onward through Kigali to Goma.

Ivan persuaded his caller and one other Belgian businessman to join him, to drive to the border at Tsatsa, about 145 kilometers northeast of Goma. When they arrived at the border, they left their car parked on the Congo side. While walking across no-man's-land in the direction of the border post on the Uganda side, several Ugandan Army trucks came barreling down on them. At least a dozen soldiers, identified by their badges as members of the Uganda Rifles of colonial days' fame, surrounded them; the soldiers were seemingly inebriated and were shouting and screaming that the three were Western spies. Ivan and his companions were rounded up and pushed toward the trucks. Some of the soldiers started hitting them with the butts of their rifles with increasing brutality. Ivan and his companions were heaved into the back of one of the trucks and beaten again with rifles. Some of the hits drew blood, and Ivan recalled that he had been frightened for a moment that the soldiers' violence would escalate. Fortunately, a senior officer had appeared, commanded the soldiers to back off, and started to interrogate the three Belgians.

Although their story was straightforward and totally believable as to why they were in that area, the officer told them that they were arrested and would be moved to Fort Portal for further interrogation and investigation. They immediately took to the road, and after a solid three-hour trip, they arrived in Fort Portal.

They were taken to a very luxurious hotel, where they were met by another senior officer, who took them into a room and continued with the interrogation. After an hour or so, they were told that they would be held captive in the hotel. Each of them was assigned a room, but they could roam freely through the hotel, partake in meals, and drink in the bar.

Yet, they were not allowed to communicate with anyone or leave the hotel premises. Ivan told me that he made friends with the Swedish hotel manager, and through him they could obtain more information. Apparently, the soldiers had overstepped their bounds with the arrest of the Belgians, but since the army did not want to look foolish, they now treated their captives as spies.

Meanwhile, a flurry of telegrams apparently went back and forth between Shell, the Ugandan government, and the Ugandan Army. This was learned from dispatches that were posted in the local newspapers and confirmed by the manager, who also obtained bits of information from the soldiers still guarding the hotel. At the end of ten days, a very senior officer from the Ugandan Rifles arrived at the hotel and commanded that the three prisoners appear in the lobby. He told them that they would be returned to the location where they had first been captured, and they were free to go their way.

Ivan did not elaborate any further, but mentioned in his closing paragraph that he had been very uncomfortable, especially during the first hour of this episode. The stay at the hotel had been comfortable, the food fine, and the bar bill truly must have been remarkable, one for the record book!

With this report finished, I turned to the letter from my father, which had taken some time to reach Bujumbura, although by now I was already accustomed to the imperfections of the African mail. In any event, he confirmed that the clothing had been sent, and the specification I had asked for was in the package, which I already had found. He further mentioned that the tennis shoes I must have found with the clothing were his, as these were accidentally packed by my mother! He was grieving about his loss, but that was Pa; he always made a mountain out of a molehill, such as his loud complaints when a button was missing from his pants. "Magda," he would exclaim to my mother for everyone to hear, "a disaster; a button is missing from my pants." Of course, this meant that my mother had to get into action immediately to repair the garment in question without delay!

nother highlight in his letter was a suggested visit he would make to my former girlfriend, Carola Cutler, and her mother while he was visiting New York for an important event for the European Investment Bank. I had not seen Carola since 1960, when I was in New York on my last trip across the Atlantic on a freighter chartered by the company my father was managing at the time. Carola had been a "steady" of mine for about a year, when I was fourteen years old. Since he was leaving in a few days, I did not bother to reply, as I assumed that he had already planned to meet Carola and her mother.

Finally, I came to a postscript in his letter; it was a well-intended lecture about how one should conduct oneself in a business situation such as the one I was in. The gist of the page-long admonishment was not to act like the new broom that sweeps clean, but rather observe and note anything that was perhaps a subject for improvement in the conduct of the business. Don't change anything immediately, he stated, and don't say anything negative about your colleague now on leave, as this might backfire on you at a later stage. It was all well-intended, but I did not particularly take to his backseat driving. I noted his concern and certainly did not entirely ignore his advice.

The day after Christmas, I arranged for a brief meeting with Ambassador Bennett, as I wished to tell him about Ivan's travails. When I arrived at his office, his secretary asked me how I had spent my Christmas holiday. I told her about my lonely enjoyment of a half bottle of scotch, whereupon she exclaimed that if I only had let her know, she would have arranged for me to be invited to one of the many parties held around town. She asked me what my plans were for New Year's Eve, whereupon I had to confess that I probably would finish the other half of the bottle of scotch in the solitude of my bungalow. Immediately, she told me that was not going to happen and that I could expect to hear from her later that day.

My meeting with Ambassador Bennett was very cordial; he thanked me for the courtesy of the information and promised that he would keep me posted on anything relevant to Shell's interest in the region. I should not hesitate to contact him whenever I needed amplification or confirmation of the many rumors bouncing around town. We parted with good wishes for the coming new year.

That very afternoon, Bennett's secretary called me and said that I was invited by the general manager of British Petroleum, Mr. Van Oeteren, to join a New Year's Eve black tie cocktail and dinner party at his home. As I had met Van Oeteren briefly through Paul's introduction, I called his office and thanked him profusely for the kind invitation.

To make sure our business was running as it should in Kigali, I booked a flight on the morning of December 28 and notified Baganzicaha about my arrival. This was my first trip in a six-person Piper Baron, owned by a small private company run by a bush pilot. Commercial flights also were available with Air Burundi flying a near-vintage DC-3 Dakota, but the bush pilot was a bit more flexible in his schedule. It was a fine day in Kigali, and we had a drink to celebrate the coming of the new year with the few employees who were around that day. I also visited with Fred Wagoner to inform him also of De Stoop's situation. Fred was very appreciative of the information and added that he already had been notified about the release of the trio.

27

Van Oeteren's New Year's Eve Party

This evening promised to be a great opportunity to meet several important people in the small-business and diplomatic community in Bujumbura. I also had a chance to wear my new tropical white tuxedo, as this was quite a formal dress event. Van Oeteren had been a longtime resident and manager and was well inserted in the network.

Upon arrival, I noted immediately that this was a well-attended evening, not only by the expat and local business community, but many government officials were invited. John Bennett also was present, and after I had my first round of introductions, he took me aside and quietly pointed out the various dignitaries present. In addition to the high level of importance of the primarily Tutsi officials, I was struck by their physical presence. The elegantly attired Tutsi women were strikingly tall with fine facial features, clearly projecting an air of nobility. Some of the Tutsi women were dressed in the latest elegance from the couturiers of Paris and Brussels, but the majority was wearing the national dress of wrapped materials with ample colors and designs, which I later learned were printed and produced by a Dutch manufacturer in the Netherlands.

The party evolved with drinks flowing freely, and a relaxed atmosphere developed among the guests, who clearly knew each other quite well, if not intimately. I enjoyed meeting some of my colleagues in the oil business; especially intriguing was my meeting with the new Mobil Oil manager, who had been transferred from his most recent post in Stanleyville. As the venue was not the right place to start a discussion about his recent experience during the rebel occupation in that city, Jean-Louis Montiel d'Aragon agreed to meet soon to exchange information.

As the evening wore on, we enjoyed an elaborate buffet, and I found myself in a quiet corner with a Belgian lady, Françoise Dujardin. We developed a conversation about her life in Burundi, and after a while we seemed to have an attraction for each other. Our discussion during the meal and the rest of the evening became playful, and no doubt the alcoholic intake allowed for a freer discourse. Toward the end of the evening, she asked if I would not mind driving her home, as she had been taken to the party by her driver, who was off for the remainder of the evening. I jumped to the occasion, and we found ourselves in my bungalow well after midnight exploring each other fully. I drove her home, but she insisted that I not stop the car to let her out, asking me to continue driving very slowly as she hopped out. She explained that she was in the process of a divorce and did not want anyone to know that she was being dropped off at her house this late at night. We exchanged telephone numbers, and she promised to call the next day to see if we could repeat our meeting, but only at the bungalow.

It was quite nice to have met a compatible female my age, and I returned to the bungalow excited after such a great evening in my new town, Bujumbura, and anticipating possibly meeting Françoise again. However, my responsibilities were broad, and I did not have time to indulge immediately in a romantic affair with a lady in the process of a divorce. Rather, I concentrated the next day on my work schedule in the office, making sure to contact Van Oeteren to thank him for the hospitality. I also made a thank-you call to John Bennett's secretary and told her that she had saved me from drinking the rest of my scotch in solitude!

28

January 1965

I planned another brief visit on January 5 to visit Kigali again to get to know my manager Baganzicaha a bit better. I intended to make sure we were on the same wavelength with our customer contacts, as well as the supplies from Kampala, which were always a bit of a headache due to the unreliable delivery schedules caused by the road conditions and the weather.

I arrived in the morning by Douglas DC-3, which was like flying in a museum piece, but these old planes were very reliable. Baganzicaha had arranged for me to spend the night at the Unilever Club. As soon as we dropped off the luggage, we started our rounds of client visits and repaired after lunch to the office to review the scheduled deliveries from Kampala.

It all seemed in order, and I paid a visit to Fred Wagoner at the US Embassy to discuss the events surrounding the Ivan de Stoop situation. Fred appreciated that I contacted him and brought him into the picture, as this was very helpful information to add to the complicated scenario regarding the situation with the border closings and the American interest in the region.

Following our discussion, I was invited to dinner, and I enjoyed a wonderful evening with him and his wife, Jane, comparing notes and talking about my previous visits to the United States. I retired to my room at the Unilever Club and fell asleep rapidly.

Sometime during the night, I woke up because an intense stench was pervading the room. I had no idea what it could be, and I opened the window, hoping this would bring a bit of relief. Instead the stench intensified, and I closed the window again and checked the time. It was three in the morning, and I was still tired. Despite the heavy odor, I fell asleep again, but by daybreak I awoke and once again noticed the stench. I decided to get up, wash, and dress, and then went to see the manager in the office. I told him about the horrendous smell, and he started laughing almost hysterically.

He took me by the arm, and we returned to my room. Outside on the small terrace I noticed a large oil drum covered by a piece of heavy material. The closer we came to the drum, the worse the smell became, and I was wondering what on earth could cause this odorous horror. The manager removed the covering cloth of the drum and, while closing his nose with his thumb and index finger of the other hand, he pointed inside and mumbled, "Look for yourself my friend!" I peeked into the barrel, also closing my nose, but the smell was worse than ever. I looked straight at the head of a buffalo, which was nearly completely submerged in water inside the barrel. The manager started laughing again while he told me the story.

A new employee of Unilever had taken a great liking to hunting, and the past weekend, right after the new year, he had been invited on a hunting trip in the east of Rwanda. He demonstrated his prowess as a hunter when he killed two charging buffaloes with two bullets from his double-barreled hunting rifle. To celebrate his triumph, he was awarded the head of one of the buffaloes, and to make sure it would be a good trophy, it had been recommended to him to bleach the head in a barrel with plenty of water.

Since the hunter did not think my cabin was occupied, the barrel had been put under the window on the small terrace in front of the cabin. I was nearly gagging again from the stench and left the premises for a last quick meeting with Fred Wagoner. Upon meeting with him, I shared the story of my experience with the stench and the resulting discovery of the buffalo's head. Fred laughed for an instant but immediately invited me to stay at their home any time I liked from now on, as he had done for Paul. I could not have found adequate words of thanks for his gracious offer, and I left town with the memory of an indelible stench but with a feeling of immense gratitude toward this kind American officer and diplomat.

Barely back from my Kigali trip, new disturbing developments came to Burundi. On January 7, the day after my return, the mwami sacked his prime minister, Alban Niamoya, as I learned from my secretary, who had her ear to the ground regarding the local gossip and rumor mill. Niamoya had been too close with the Chinese, whose presence and influence in Burundi had earned him the mwami's scorn. He was replaced by a moderate former prime minister, Pierre Ngendandumwe. I immediately put in a call to John Bennett at the UK Embassy and asked him for the reason and the implications of this move by the Burundi king.[20]

---

[20] Sacking of Alban Niamoya, Prime Minister Burundi, and Chinese communist influence in Burundi http://www.arib. info/index.php?option=com_content&task=view&id=1379.

29

Bujumbura Golf Club—Meeting Mobil Oil Manager —Account of Stanleyville's Rebel Occupation

Having returned to Burundi, I spent the weekend at the golf club and had the opportunity to meet informally with my newly arrived colleague from Mobil Oil, Jean-Louis Montiel d'Aragon, who I had just met at the New Year's Eve party at Van Oeteren. We played nine holes on the course, where the fifth hole wrapped around the gardens of the mwami's presidential grounds. This was a very tricky hole, as one could either play it safe and go straight with a soft iron shot and then directly at a ninety-degree angle into the green, or take the risky, but sure bet, birdie approach, which was a direct angled shot across a corner of the mwami's garden and land the ball close to the green, or with some luck even on the green. The risk was to miss the shot and land the ball within the enclosure of the mwami's grounds; this is when it became a tricky situation.

One could either climb across the two-meter-high fence, search for the ball and risk being taken into custody by the palace guards, or one could call out to the guards, hope that they would be close and ask them (for a small consideration) to retrieve your ball, toss it across the fence, and you would take the penalty for an out-of-bounds ball and continue. I was assured by my playing partner that this was a safer way, and probably the best way, to go.

After our round of golf, Jean-Louis and I spent time on the golf club's terrace consuming the omnipresent Primus beer. Jean-Louis had only recently arrived in Bujumbura after spending considerable time in Stanleyville. It was fascinating to listen to his account of the invasion of the Simbas in Stanleyville. He had been in his penthouse apartment off the main street, when he witnessed the rebels approaching the Congolese Army, which had been to the right of his vantage point on the terrace of his penthouse. The government troops had been heavily armed, dressed in army fatigues, and lined up to fire machine guns of various calibers down the street toward any approaching rebel contingent. While Jean-Louis was getting increasingly anxious watching the army, he could see the rebels in the far distance approaching.

They were a ragtag band of undisciplined followers of Mulele, but they were all determined to progress toward their next objective, the capture of Stanleyville. These "warriors" has been drugged with *dagga*, a stimulant derived from a mint-related plant that produces psychotic reactions in the user. In addition, these troops, who, as already mentioned, had animistic beliefs, had been told by their witch doctors that they would be immune to bullets if they continuously sprinkled themselves with water while singing the praise of Mulele. Jean-Louis could not believe his eyes when the

Simbas came trotting and dancing down the boulevard, singing in loud voices: "Mai, Mulele; Mai, Mulele" while waving branches across themselves after dipping them in buckets of water. They advanced toward the Congolese Army soldiers on the other end, who were hiding behind their fortifications that spanned the street. Everything was quiet except for the singing and rustling of the advancing mass of rebels. Suddenly, at three hundred meters, the army opened fire pointblank at the rebels.

Jean-Louis recalled his amazement and horror when the bullets ripped into the first line of rebels, felling and killing a great number of them. But the scary part was that some of them who were wounded by bullets, leaving large holes in their bodies, continued to walk forward as if nothing had happened, advancing at ever-increasing speed. A second burst of machine-gun fire toppled another group of rebels, but again a wounded, bleeding row of wide-eyed Simbas kept walking like zombies toward the army troops. As they approached the barricades within a few hundred meters, suddenly the soldiers dropped their guns, abandoned their positions and started to run away from their line of defense. Several climbed into jeeps and trucks and made off with a loud roar toward the western end of town, not to be seen again.

The rebels exploded into an even-wilder moving bunch, celebrating their clear victory despite leaving behind hundreds of dead and wounded in the wake of their attack. I sat there on the terrace, mesmerized by Jean-Louis's story and wondering how he had ever gotten out of the town during the days that followed. He apparently had stayed in his apartment without being detected, and after the liberation of the captured Europeans by the Belgian paratroopers, he joined the exodus from town to Léopoldville. After a brief period of rest and recuperation, Mobil reassigned him to Burundi as its general manager for the region.

During the next few months, I would learn more about the massacres that had taken place in Rwanda in 1959 from tales told by two UN representatives I happened to meet in town. They had been in Bujumbura at the time of the slaughter of some hundred thousand Tutsis in Rwanda at the hands of the Hutu majority following an assassination attempt on the then prime minister. They had been told to go to the bridge across the Ruzizi River just northeast of Bujumbura. When they arrived, they noticed a few boys loitering at the bridge. The boys offered to show them bodies in the river for a *matabish*, a payment. Some of the badly decomposed human remains were pulled by rope to the shore. In the days following, the UN representatives returned a few times and witnessed a pink tinge to the flowing river—blood. More bodies came floating down, mutilated by blows from machetes and often torn apart by crocodiles.

30

The Rwanda Massacres

One of my clients, a tall and striking Tutsi, explained to me one day when I asked him offhandedly about the strife between the Hutus and the Tutsis, that in Rwanda the Tutsis had been the rulers, the aristocracy, and lived in the middle of many kraals, or rural villages. Once the attacks started on the Tutsis, all the Hutus had to do was to enter the center of the kraal and slaughter the defenseless Tutsis gathered there. After the initial attacks subsided, close to two hundred thousand Tutsis escaped the country to continue their opposition from outside Rwanda.

I asked my client why this slaughter had not happened in Burundi. He explained that in Burundi it was not as easy for the Hutus to attack the Tutsis, because they controlled the army through the mwami and because they were not living in the middle of kraals, but were spread through the country and therefore could not be easily targeted. I felt that this information should be conveyed to my general manager, and I wrote an elaborate report about my findings. I am sure that he was fully informed about the Stanleyville story, but in a response to my report, De Freitas asked me to continue to report these kinds of stories to him if I felt that they might add to his understanding of the situation of our business in my region.

31

Ita Komanski #1

One evening I was invited by a British national about my age to join him for drinks at the only nightclub attended by Europeans in Bujumbura. Since the assassination of Ngendandumwe, the club had been closed due to the curfew imposed on the country. However, the curfew had been relaxed, and we could visit this usually well-attended establishment until ten in the evening.

It was a very quiet evening, as it was the middle of the week, but in one of the corners in the back, I noted that the mwami was present with his French mistress. The mwami was a rather worldly individual, who spent quite a bit of time in Europe and was reputed to love visiting nightclubs.

At the bar, I noticed a threesome of two Belgians I was vaguely familiar with, who were accompanying a strikingly beautiful woman. I could not help but let my eyes wander toward her reflection in the big mirror behind the bar. She had dark hair worn in a short bouffant style; remarkable was a streak of natural gray hair, which extended from the middle of her forehead toward the middle of her head. She had very delicate features and was in an animated discussion with her companions. I tried not to be impolite and diverted my glances to the back of the room, where I saw the mwami much involved in a discussion with his paramour, Françoise.

I vaguely noted the rather uninteresting commentary of my English companion about the developments in the country and nodded my agreement with his statements about the recent expulsion of the Chinese from Burundi and the political implications this would entail for the country. I glanced again toward my left and caught the eyes of this wonderful creature at the bar. I was wondering if she was a local, or whether she might be visiting Bujumbura. The evening progressed, and before the start of curfew, we left the bar to return to our respective homes. I still could not get the image of this gorgeous lady out of my head, but soon enough I was taken in Morpheus's arms for a peaceful rest.

The next day, I went to the office at my regular hour. It must have been around ten o'clock, when my secretary opened the door of my office, and before she could announce the visitor, Ivan de Stoop nearly fell into the room. I jumped to my feet, a bit startled to see him so unexpectedly. Ivan explained that he had taken a few days off to visit Bujumbura on a private trip and that he was returning the next day to Goma. I asked him to explain why he had driven all the way from Goma to Bujumbura for a vacation.

Without a word, he went to my window and pulled aside the curtain, pointing to his Volkswagen parked outside. I nearly gagged because inside the car I recognized the same gorgeous woman I had noticed the evening before in the nightclub. She was not aware that we were looking at her, and after I closed the curtain, I asked Ivan who his companion might be. Ivan had met her in Goma, where she was in a relationship with a Belgian planter, having divorced her first husband. She had been visiting Bujumbura to arrange for papers that pertained to her divorce, which apparently had been a rather messy affair. Ivan told me that she had asked him to pick her up and take her back to Goma, as she could not get an easy connection back by air. I did not ask any further questions, but I suspected that Ivan must have had a more involved relationship with the lady.

I asked him for her name, and Ivan said it was Ita Komanski and explained that she was a Belgian national, but of Russian ancestry. She apparently had settled in Goma with her first husband, a trader, and remained there following her divorce. Ivan invited me to follow him to his car so he could introduce me to her.

With great excitement, I went outside. She opened the car window: "Ita Komanski," she said, and she promptly apologized not to be able to stay much longer in Bujumbura. Surprisingly, she mentioned that she had noticed me the evening before at the nightclub. I asked her to forgive my impolite glancing at her that previous evening, but she waved it away and said that she hoped to meet me again. I gave her my business card and told her to just let me know when she might be in town again and that I would be delighted to help her in any way, shape, or form, if so required. Ivan joined her in the car, and with a final big smile on his face, bade his farewell to me. I had another long look at this spectacular woman as Ivan turned the car into the street and drove away. I wondered if I would ever see her again, and, in a semitrance, I returned to my office.

32

Rising Waters of Lake Tanganyika— LPG Container Shortage

As if the recent political uproar were not already enough to keep one's blood flowing during recent months, the area toward Kigoma in Kenya had been flooded. My supplies of gasoline, diesel fuel, and LPG canisters were shipped from Mombasa by rail to Kigoma and from there by barge or lake tanker to Bujumbura, and the shipments had been affected by the floods.

Lake Tanganyika had been rising steadily, and we were told that the delivery of our supplies might be interrupted if the floods continued for much longer. It would not be long before the barges and tankers could not be loaded at the quays in Kigoma, and those already on the way to Bujumbura would have to be anchored out of town. As it happened, we had an ample supply of gasoline and diesel in our onshore tanks, but the available supply of full LPG canisters was very low for all oil companies. I began to receive calls from my clients that they were in dire need of the fifty-pound canisters used for household cooking gas. I called around to my colleagues at the other oil companies, and invariably I received the message that they were also out of stock or nearly so.

Just at that time, I received a phone call from a Greek trader who I had met through Paul, who mentioned that he was aware of the dire situation with the stock of fifty-pound LPG canisters; he also knew that I had an ample stock of empty canisters, so he made an interesting proposal. He somehow had in his possession the equipment needed to decant gas from one-hundred-pound canisters to fifty-pounders; he would be delighted to help Shell if he would get a discount on his purchases once the gas had been transferred to the smaller canisters.

Although I was aware of the Shell regulations that decanting was prohibited other than through Shell personnel or those licensed by Shell to perform this kind of work, I immediately asked him to come to my office to discuss this matter. As the communications with our head office were dismal, and a formal approval would take weeks to obtain, I decided to take the risk and made a deal with the Greek. Thus, I could offer fifty-pound canisters not only to my own distributors, but also to plenty of clients of my competitors, all of whom were out of fifty-pound supplies.

In the ensuing weeks, I broke all sales records for LPG, made a lot of people very happy, avoided a crisis in many a household for a potential lack of cooking gas, and my Greek connection made a few extra francs for his ingenious offer. Even a few of my competitors called me to compliment me on my ingenuity, as they were too happy to see their clients bailed out during this difficult time.

While telling about our LPG canisters stored at our out-of-town depot, I should relate another issue about the safety conditions of our depots. The depot in town, where we stored mostly our lubricants and other packaged products, did not provide any difficulties. We had guards staying day and night in the building, which was securely locked from the inside. However, our depot about five kilometers out of town was in an uninhabited area surrounded by open fields and only reachable by a dirt road, and was potentially more vulnerable. Although we had guards rotating at this facility, one could never be sure about their vigilance and adherence to our rules to be always awake and to keep a close eye on the surrounding area.

At night, the depot was lighted, albeit with too few lamps to make a real difference, but Paul had suggested that I continue with his practice to visit both the town depot and the out-of-town one on a regular basis, but at variable intervals, so the guards would not be able to predict our arrival. I had followed this sensible instruction, but because of the curfew upon us, I had a hard time going around town at night. My Italian transporter came to the rescue, as he offered to lend me a well-used Jeep to allow me to drive around after curfew and appear to be one of the Belgian military officers, who were not restricted by the curfew.

I disguised myself to look like a Belgian officer by wearing a khaki bush outfit and donned my black beret with the insignia of my Dutch regiment, the Hussars of Boreel, which I had kept with me as a souvenir of my days in the army in the Netherlands. As soon as it was dark, I proceeded on my way to visit the depots on an irregular basis. I passed other military vehicles at times, but no one stopped me or even acknowledged my presence.

For the next few months, I kept my vigil going. The guards clearly were quite uncertain as to my arrival and would, as far as I knew, at least be a bit more awake during their guarding hours. This action had been necessary, contrary probably to all rules and regulations, but once again, I had my responsibilities to secure Shell property, so I did what I could under the circumstances to make sure that our operations would not be adversely affected.

33

Annual Contract Allocation
with the Rwanda Government

Once a year, the oil companies submitted a tender offer to the government of Rwanda for all their required supplies of gasoline. It had become customary that the five managers of the oil companies would fly together to Kigali from Bujumbura to submit the necessary documentation. We all knew in advance which of the five would be awarded the supplies for the next year, as the pricing had already been arranged through our respective head offices in Europe and the United States. In any event, we had to go through this charade and charter a private bush plane, a six-seater Piper Baron.

The trip to Kigali was uneventful, and we took a car, arranged in advance by my representative, to the government offices, submitted our papers, and returned to the airport an hour later. The flight back took the customary fifty minutes, and we saw the airport clearly, with a long runway, ahead of us. At that point, our pilot seemed somewhat agitated and started to mumble that we might have a problem with our landing gear, as an alarm indicator turned red, which could mean that the gear was not properly locking into place. With a series of expletives, he pulled up the landing gear and reported the problem to the control tower, while he regained altitude. The tower instructed him to turn back to the airport and fly around the tower while lowering the landing gear, so they could have a visual look to see whether the gear descended or not. Meanwhile, the tension in the aircraft could be cut with a knife, and my companion in the seat next to me, the manager of Total, turned an ashen gray and was mumbling some prayers under his breath. I found the situation quite interesting, and I was following the pilot's conversation with the tower with great excitement.

The pilot seemed very competent, a real bush pilot, who was not going to be thrown off by some technical problem. He started to tell us that he would make another attempt after the tower confirmed that the landing gear had properly descended. The tower gave him approval for an attempt to land with the instruction to come in at a slightly higher speed, allowing him to abort the landing if for any reason the landing gear collapsed or retracted.

At this point my companion was completely panicked. He grabbed a bag, and I thought he was about to throw up, when the pilot touched the runway and slowly began lowering the plane to the ground. It turned out that a small electrical failure had prompted the red light to come on, causing the incorrect indication of a landing gear failure. We all exited the plane with another adventure for the books. We took the pilot to a local bar and celebrated his capabilities.

Of course, he started to regale us with plenty of stories concerning his experiences as a bush pilot. It was here that many a beer and whiskey were consumed, and we returned to our homes inebriated but happy at the outcome of this adventure.

This event would not be my last incident with air travel. One day on one of my flights to Kigali, this time with the regularly scheduled flight of Air Burundi in their DC-3 Dakota, I was warned that the flight pattern had been changed, but that there was no reason for alarm. In the past, the plane would have taken off from the airport and turned west in the direction of the Congolese border before heading north to Kigali, but this time we were going to swing east across to the lake and then head north. I wasn't too concerned but asked the airline representative what the reason was for this change in flight pattern. He explained that in the past few weeks, the Congolese rebels had been taking potshots at the departing planes when they had come close to the Congolese border before turning north. No plane had been hit, but the risks were too great to continue the traditional approach, and hence the change in the flight pattern. Now that I had become an old hand in the region, I just brushed it off as another passing event and happily continued flying the DC-3 to Kigali.

34

Ita Komanski #2

A few days after my return from that trip, I received a telephone call from someone at the airport. My secretary could not tell me who was on the phone, other than that it was a female who was urgently asking to talk to me. I took the call, and, to my utter surprise, Ita Komanski announced her arrival at the Bujumbura airport from Goma. I was astounded to hear her voice, and at her request I hurried there to pick her up.

I was very excited to see this beautiful woman again, but I had no idea why she had called me instead of her local connections. As she explained on our trip to town, she had returned to Bujumbura to deal with some additional urgent legal matters, and she had not been able to plan to be picked up at the airport. So, she had decided to call me, as she was sure that I would not mind assisting her, based on our brief meeting a few weeks earlier. Of course, I told her it was a pleasure to help her while she was visiting, and I took her to the Palace Hotel, where she had arranged for a room.

As she had some meetings that very afternoon and was busy with the lawyers through that evening, I arranged for my driver Oscar to take her around town and told her I would meet her again the next morning. The next day, prior to going to my office, I stopped by the Palace Hotel and called her room. She asked me to come upstairs, and when I knocked on her door, she asked me to come in. I was utterly surprised when I saw her at the dressing table partially dressed. She apologized for her semi-dressed state, but told me she was in a hurry to go to the lawyers again that very morning and would not be free until later for lunch. Of course, I immediately asked her to join me for lunch, and we met later that day at my favorite restaurant. I was taken with her, as I had been during our first encounter in the nightclub.

She had a very easy manner, and her conversation was sparkling and intelligent. She told me that she had to stay another couple of days in Bujumbura while her lawyers completed certain documents that required more time than was anticipated. I asked her if I could offer her a bedroom at my bungalow, so she would not have to stay in the dingy Palace Hotel. She accepted immediately, and I promised to pick her up late that afternoon. So, I did, and we went to my residence. In the interim, I had arranged for the main bedroom in the house to be aired and cleaned, with some fresh flowers adorning the dresser.

She was obviously much taken with my hospitality, and we spent the rest of the evening enjoying a light meal prepared by my houseboy/cook and imbibing some very nice French wine. She told me that she was divorced and had three children by her first husband. Sadly, one of her kids had drowned in a swimming pool, which clearly affected her greatly. I told her the story of my brother Rem, who had been killed in a skiing accident at the age of sixteen.

I related the impact his passing had made on all our family, but especially on my mother, who had not yet fully recovered from his death. This discussion seemed to further bond us, and we spent the rest of the time talking about our past, but I had some difficulty extracting her true story. Yet, it did not matter to me, as just being with her was a treat. We spent that night in harmony exploring each other, enjoying the close quarters of the main bedroom enhanced by the idyllic tropical noises that engulfed the house.

She stayed another four days, and I arranged for a small party with a group of single Belgians I had met in town during the last several months. It turned out to be a delightful evening, with all of us enjoying fine wine, good food, and lots of dancing. At the end of the evening, well after curfew had started, my guests were escorted home by one of my guests, a Belgian army officer who was permitted to travel at any time around town. Due to his presence, the escorting of my guests had allowed for a truly splendid and late evening.

The Belgian officer with friends

More friends dancing?!

It was as if we had always been together, and the day I drove her back to the airport was one of joy and of sadness. Her business had been concluded, and I knew when I bade her farewell at the airport that we would never see each other again. This encounter made me long for a more permanent relationship. I was beginning to seriously think about meeting some ladies upon the conclusion of my first tour for Shell during my home leave of two months and considering marriage again.

35

Border Closing Threat between Uganda and Rwanda

It had been quite a few days, and I was finally finding time to address my administrative work, which Paul had told me must be kept up to date. My sales results had been well above target, and the LPG caper had been particularly profitable. As I was updating the budget books, my secretary came hurriedly into my office: "Ivan is on the phone. He needs to talk to you immediately!" We had never managed to get a decent connection, and I could barely hear him on the other end. "We have to meet tomorrow," he yelled into the phone. "Why, Ivan?" I asked. Over the noisy line, he managed to tell me that there were potential problems, with the Uganda government threatening to close the borders between Rwanda and Uganda. He said he would send a telex explaining the problems he had become aware of in discussions with other businesspeople in Goma.

His telex arrived, and it was quite alarming. If the borders were closed, we would have a major problem supplying our customers in Rwanda, as well as in Goma, which had been supplied by Shell Uganda by sending trucks through Rwanda since the borders had been closed for some time between Uganda and eastern Congo. I replied by telex that I would leave that very afternoon for Kigali by road with Oscar, our driver, spend the night with Fred Wagoner, who I had already notified by telex, and continue the next morning around eight, and that we would meet each other on the Ruhengeri Road anywhere between Ruhengeri and Goma. We agreed on this plan, and I called Ambassador Bennett to ask him for an immediate meeting. Bennett was not aware of any border closing rumor and asked me what the implications might be for the supply of Rwanda and Goma by Shell.

I told him in strict confidence that Shell was the only oil company with any storage capacity in our depot in Kigali. I added that this was a limited amount of ten thousand gallons, barely enough for a few days' supply. I told him about my plan to meet with Ivan de Stoop the next day on the road and to proceed with him to the border with Uganda at Cyanika to assess the situation on the spot.

I departed an hour later and left the driving to Oscar, a truly expert driver on the miserable dirt roads leading to Kigali. I had no problem passing the military and customs border controls, as I had obtained passes to let me through, since Shell represented a vital element for the oil supplies in both countries. That evening I arrived at the Wagoners' residence around dinnertime. I was led into the house by a houseboy and told that Fred was awaiting me in the dining room. Upon entering, I was totally surprised; sitting at the table with a big smile on his face was John Bennett. After my initial surprise, John said in his inimitable British accent:

"Well, Hans, I thought it would be interesting to hear what your further plans were going to be in relation to a potential border closing, so I imposed on Fred to join you both for dinner!"

We immediately started to review the known facts, which were limited mainly to the statements by Ivan de Stoop. Fred asked me what we would do if indeed the borders were closed. He mentioned very confidentially that the United States had committed to the Rwanda government to assist in bringing supplies of gasoline to the country by air. However, he stated that such support would have great political and diplomatic consequences, so anything that could be done to avoid US involvement would be extremely helpful. I stated that I would not be able to give any answer to the question of future supplies by Shell, as I would first have to assess the situation the next day. However, I promised to inform Fred as soon as we had any idea of our next moves. Both men probed me again on the available storage capacity of Shell and the other oil companies in Rwanda.

As I had already explained to John Bennett in Bujumbura that very morning, Shell was the only petroleum company in Rwanda with some underground storage and that was limited to a ten-thousand-gallon tank. The additional storage was disbursed among the various gasoline stations, but in total this would probably amount to not more than an additional twenty thousand gallons of storage capacity, which might not have been filled to the rim. I was questioned about the supply time from Kampala to Kigali and possibly onward to Goma, and I told them what I could, based on the current estimated transportation times.

We concluded the evening with some conversation about the current political mess in the region, and I elaborated a bit on my Shell colleagues' stories about the recent turmoil in Stanleyville. The evening concluded with John Bennett returning on his chartered flight back to Bujumbura and my retreating to the guest quarters at Fred's residence for a good night's sleep.

The next morning, Oscar and I hit the road again at eight in the morning. We drove for several hours, passing the town of Ruhengeri, and took the road toward Gisenyi and Goma. We had been driving on the slippery dirt road for some four hours when a dust cloud approached us from the opposite direction. We passed each other, and the other car started honking wildly. Oscar and I realized immediately that the car was Ivan's, and we stopped, turned around, and joined his Volkswagen Beetle, now stopped on the road. Jumping out of our cars, we shook hands, and Ivan immediately suggested that we drive the opposite direction back to Ruhengeri and on to the border post at Cyanika. He had no further information, and the only way we would be able to know the next move of the government in Kampala would be to ask the border police.

Ivan took the lead, and we drove in tandem to the border, but we decided to stop short of the border and leave Oscar at a reasonable distance waiting for us. As he was a Congolese, he would not be too welcomed by the Ugandans! I put my maps and camera into Ivan's Beetle, and onward we went to the border post. An impressive-looking Ugandan officer stopped us and ordered us to get out of the vehicle while he inspected the car. We had not been able to even identify ourselves, before he drew his revolver and pointed it at us with the words: "You two are spies!" Ivan mumbled that we were businessmen and needed information, but the officer opened the car and took our maps and my camera and proceeded to wave these in our faces, shouting "Why do you need all those maps, and what are you doing with this camera?" Once again, we told him that we were employees of Royal Dutch Shell and that we needed information. He seemed to calm down, putting his revolver back into the holster.

He proclaimed that he would empty the camera, and after returning the maps to our car, he opened the camera and took out the film, which he put in his pocket. "Now," he asked, "what is it you need to know?" Ivan calmly explained that we had heard multiple rumors that the border between Uganda and Rwanda would be closed to all traffic and requested that he please tell us if this was correct and, if so, when the border closing would go into effect. The officer took another long look at us and requested to see our passports and our Shell identification.

Apparently assured that we were legitimate, he told us that the instructions had been issued from the president's office and confirmed by the army headquarters in Kampala that the borders would be closed in ten days' time. Ivan and I conferred and decided on the spot to continue our trip to Kampala. It was of utmost importance to get our gasoline supplies moving toward Kigali as soon as possible.

The fastest and most efficient way would be for us to drive to Kampala and discuss the situation with Shell Uganda representatives to assure that we could get enough trucks on the road to establish an emergency supply in our depot in Kigali. We would instruct our transporters in Kampala to get as many trucks on the road as possible and leave them stationed fully loaded in our depot until the crisis had passed.

If this action was successful, and the border closure was not too long, we would have enough gasoline to weather the storm and supply both Rwanda and Goma for a few weeks. We also knew that we would be the sole suppliers of gasoline during that period, allowing us to make a killing in the market, as our competitors had no supplies in the country. They would not be aware of our arrangements before they could get into action, and we would already have cornered the market with our supply train of trucks.

Ivan and I wrote out the texts of several telexes to our head office in Léopoldville, our respective offices in Bujumbura and Goma, and I wrote a note to Fred Wagoner explaining the situation and our anticipated actions. I also requested him to send that information to John Bennett in Bujumbura. Ivan and I knew full well that we should obtain formal approval first from the head office in Léo before officially traveling to a neighboring country on business. However, immediate communications were impossible, as there were no telephones, nor a telex facility available. We decided to act on our own volition and face any potential disciplinary consequences or criticism upon our return.

36

From Cyanika to Kampala

The route to Kampala was all *marrum* roads, a compacted soil that was relatively easy to drive on in dry conditions, except for the clouds of dust that would follow cars all along their path. However, when the rains came, *marrum* roads would be like skating rinks, requiring advanced driving skills to keep a car on the road. Such was our luck after we left Cyanika. The skies opened, and the next two hours of driving were sheer hell for the driver, my colleague Ivan, poor guy. But once the rain stopped, he took a stroll around the car, and with a sigh he said that the next few hours would be mine at the wheel.

I was not entirely comfortable with his suggestion because I had never driven a right-side driver car before. I took to the road and immediately felt its slickness, but managed to keep the car under control for the next half hour. However, we were on a very hilly stretch with lots of curves, and as I approached a very steep one, I felt the rear of the Beetle moving away from me. I had a lot of experience driving a Beetle in the Netherlands and knew that the heavy backend tended to slip away. But with a slight correction, especially on a dry road, the Beetle would normally respond and straighten out beautifully. However, this was not a nice dry road; this was *marrum*, wet and slick, so when I corrected the sliding car, I overcorrected because of my unfamiliarity with the right-hand drive. Immediately the Beetle went into a skid just as I came into a nasty turn in the road. I lost control, and the Beetle continued a straight line toward the side of the road and then abruptly continued downward at a sixty-degree angle for at least three meters. It bobbed up and down and turned on its two right wheels, ever continuing in a straight line.

I heard cursing from Ivan, and the door on my side opened and banged closed again against the side of my head. Now the car shifted onto the left two wheels, slowing down appreciably, but not enough to stop it entirely. Then it shifted back with a loud bang on all four wheels and with a last gasp came to a halt against an embankment, some fifteen feet below the road. I quickly got out of the car and saw Ivan also emerging from the rather crumpled Beetle.

We looked at each other with astonishment that we had escaped from this wild ride with just a small amount of blood on my face from a scratch caused by the closing door that had slammed against my glasses. Amazingly, the glasses had survived, and Ivan and I were not hurt. However, the seam of the seat of my pants had ripped. The Beetle, slightly shortened, seemed only mildly damaged.

Within fifteen minutes or so, and out of nowhere, we were surrounded by no less than twenty Ugandans, talking to each other and pointing at the car and us. One of them approached us and asked if they could be of help and if we had any injuries. Confirming that we had no more than my scratch, we mentioned that if they could get the car back onto the road, we would be extremely grateful.

Clearly, this gentleman was the leader, and with a few commands he marshaled some ten of his compatriots to lift and gently carry the damaged vehicle up a slight incline to the main road. We watched the proceedings in great awe; it was hard to believe that half an hour after our crash the car was back on the road.

We inspected the damage and, although the front of the car had been pushed inward and upward, we managed to open the cover of the engine compartment in the back. After pushing the bumper and the cover back with the handle of the jack, Ivan started the motor, and, to our utter amazement, the car came to life, although it was emitting a suspicious amount of smoke.

The leader of the Africans told us that the next village would be Bubale and that we would find a mechanic in the town who could assess the damage. We profusely thanked our band of rescuers, and, leaving some money with the leader for their extraordinary help, we jumped in the beaten-up Beetle and started down the road to Bubale.

With an increasingly smoking engine, we arrived about twenty minutes later at this small town. I noted a sign, almost by accident, of an Indian tailor and asked Ivan to stop so I could get help for my split pants. While I was trying to have my pants mended, Ivan went down the street looking for someone to give a diagnosis for the Beetle.

I climbed up the stairs to the elevated shop and found an Indian tailor inside. I pointed to my split pants and asked him if he could repair them right away. He pointed to the door and said I could undo my pants behind it and hand them to him. I had not counted on the gang of young boys now gathering around this white visitor. They were pointing at my damaged pants, and when I went behind the door and handed my pants to the tailor, they broke into a loud cheer and laughter.

Standing there in my underpants, I had to laugh with them, and after the repair had been made, I emerged from behind the door and gave my supporters a few coins to make them happy. They cheered again, and I proceeded to take a few bows, as if I was a stage performer! At least, my pants were once more in presentable condition.

As if by a miracle, Ivan had found a repair shop, also run by a few Indians, but the diagnosis was not in our favor, and we had to admit that the Beetle was a write-off. Ivan was not too concerned, as the rented and well-insured VW could be left behind, and it would be returned to Goma through the courtesy of the rental company. Meanwhile, the urgency of our trip to Kampala had not diminished.

The owner of the repair shop called his brother, who was surprisingly an instant cab driver and who was willing to drive us to Kampala for a fair price. He drove us the remaining three hundred-odd kilometers, and we enjoyed the sights of the mountain range and other scenic vistas during the remainder of the trip. We arrived finally in the late afternoon at Shell House in Kampala.

We immediately had a meeting with the general manager and the operations manager, who contacted our Italian transporter, who was under contract to make all the supply trips for Shell to Kigali and Goma. After considerable discussion and terrific support from our Shell colleagues, we were assured that the first truck would be leaving that very afternoon and that for the next ten days they would put as many trucks on the road to our depot in Kigali as they could muster. We sent another telex to Léo head office to tell them about our actions, progress, and itinerary. We also accepted the invitation from our transporter, who was delighted by this unexpected windfall, to join him for dinner that evening. Meanwhile, Ivan had arranged to rent another Beetle in the interim. It was unreal how, after all the driving, the accident, and the taxi ride to Kampala, we had accomplished our entire objective in just a few hours.

All of this also was happening on a Friday, so we had the entire weekend to return to Kigali, meet with Oscar, and spend time with Fred Wagoner to brief him fully on the latest developments. Ivan suggested that we drive that very evening after dinner to a hotel on the way to Fort Portal, as he wanted me to see where he had been held under house arrest a few months earlier, and meet with the Swedish manager. On our return from Fort Portal, we could take the route through the Queen Elizabeth Game Reserve and see some game in the process of our return trip to Kigali.

Following a splendid Italian meal at the house of our truck contractor's mother, we proceeded for yet a few more hours on the road to Fort Portal. When we finally crashed in our beds, we had no problem falling into a deep sleep. Refreshed, we continued our way early the next morning to Fort Portal.

37

Fort Portal and Queen Elizabeth National Park at Lake King Edward

The previous evening, we had driven roughly one hundred kilometers to the hotel where we stayed, and the next day we added another two hundred kilometers on our drive to Fort Portal. We arrived around lunchtime, and upon reaching the hotel's lobby, a blond Swede, the general manager Ivan had told me about, came enthusiastically running toward Ivan: "You made it back here. What a pleasure to see you. And how long will you be here?"

Ivan quickly brought him up to date, and in return, the Swede had a surprise for Ivan. "You know, after you left with your compatriots, not only did Shell pay for your stay in the hotel, but the Ugandan government also paid for your hotel charges, so you are most welcome to return here any time you like and consume the extras paid!" Ivan told him that he might just do that in the future.

We had a nice and tasteful lunch at the hotel, and after some advice from the Swede as to the best road to take to the park, as well as a good suggestion about where we should spend the night, we left midafternoon. Arriving at the Queen Elizabeth Park, we found a nice lodge, as the Swede had suggested, and spent the night in blissful peace after a drive through some of the park that late afternoon.

The next morning, we took a boat down the Kazinga Channel, a thirty-two-kilometer-long (twenty-mile) natural channel that links Lake Edward and Lake George and is a dominant feature of Queen Elizabeth National Park. Lake George is small, with an average depth of only 2.4 meters (7.9 feet) and is fed by streams from the Ruwenzori Mountains. Its outflow is through the Kazinga Channel, which drains into Lake Edward; its water levels fluctuate very little.[21]

Lioness resting on the banks of the Kazinga Channel

---

[21] For detailed information, visit the following link: http://www.queenelizabethnationalpark.com/kazinga-channel.html.

Hippos emerging from the channel

We watched a variety of game on the shores and saw plenty of animals both in and outside the waters. Ivan had an opportunity to tell me some of his experiences while dealing with petroleum supplies to the Congo government. Due to the rebel activities, his territory had been split, and while he was still supplying the government in the north, he had to drive through rebel territory to meet with his government clients. To appease the rebels in the event he was stopped on the road, he carried a supply of guns and radios in the back seat of his Volkswagen as a potential bribe to let him pass through their territory. He was lucky never to encounter any rebels and had continued to supply the government troops through a circuitous route.

One day, when returning from one of those trips, he thought he saw a low-hanging branch, and just as he was slowing down to avoid crashing into this limb, it rose to the sky, as an elephant showed his long ivory tusks just above the roof of his VW! Having heard bush stories before, I was not sure if I could believe these tales, but he was not the only one who had strange encounters in the jungles of the Congo, so I gave him the benefit of the doubt, while enjoying every minute of his stories.

We returned to Kigali on Sunday afternoon, about a two-hundred-kilometer drive once again on *marrum* roads, but on dry ones this time. We arrived in time for dinner at Fred Wagoner's home, and he and his wife, Jane, welcomed us both as long-lost friends. Fred said that they had been concerned about our travels and doings in Uganda, as the situation seemed quite tense. His sources had confirmed our report about the potential of the border closing. We briefed Fred on our adventure, and he said he thought we were fools. But he was also very pleased to learn that we had found a solution for the potential shortfall of gasoline. The next day, Ivan returned to Goma, assuring me that he would stay on the road and advise me of his arrival. Oscar safely returned me to Bujumbura, where I found a flood of telexes from Léo dealing with my unauthorized trip. Yet, I was told by De Freitas directly that he had heard through the British Embassy that we had done a heroic job in making our decisions that would assure a continuous supply stream for Rwanda and Goma. The dreaded "punishment" De Stoop and I had feared was converted to praise and thanks for our initiative.

38

Visits by Shell Kenya General Manager and Senior Staff

The next week, after the closing of the borders between Uganda and Rwanda, was a great one for our sales in Rwanda. I had to add a special page on top of the graphic that Paul Bröcker had prepared in his statistical sales book, as the sales ran off the page and into the stratosphere for our small organization there. Our sales representative was on the telex daily extolling the success of our gasoline sales.

We managed to supply all the customers of the other oil companies, and two special trucks were running a shuttle to Goma to assist Ivan with his sales requirements. After two weeks of diplomatic consultations and various mediations from Western countries, the borders were reopened. During their closure, we had taken full advantage of this unusual situation by grabbing the bull by the horns and making decisions contrary to the "Shell Book of Rules."

It was not until I returned to Léo that George de Freitas, our general manager, expressed his appreciation for Ivan's and my actions during this politically difficult time. I also learned from Fred Wagoner that what we did had not gone unnoticed in a variety of reports to several foreign offices abroad.

After this episode, I was bombarded by congratulatory telexes from my Shell colleagues in Kenya, who had been involved with the perilous supply problems due to the floods in the Kigoma region. They were also fully aware of the events that took place with the border closing between Rwanda, and the solutions Ivan and I had arranged. The general manager and his sales and operations managers came to Bujumbura to discuss the situation concerning the supply streams and future potential difficulties if the waters of the lake rose again, or if the railway operations were again suspended in Kenya to disrupt the supplies flowing from Mombasa to Kigoma.

Of course, I was honored to be asked to host the party from Kenya Shell, and I did everything I could to make sure that the gentlemen were received in style, but also that they would have a chance to discuss these problems with my oil company colleagues, as far as our joint storage facilities were concerned. I also arranged for the visitors to be received by John Bennett, who, as the ambassador of Great Britain, would give them an overview of the political and diplomatic situation in Burundi, especially important since the forced departure of the Chinese.

I invited a few businessmen to a small cocktail party at my home and provided an opportunity for the delegation to informally talk about the regional problems regarding the effects of the climate, as well as the current tensions within the country following the assassination of Pierre Ngendandumwe. After three days, the gentlemen returned to

Nairobi, and a glowing thank-you note from the Shell Kenya GM was enough for me to know that besides accomplishing a lot, we had also established a warm relationship with our suppliers and company colleagues in our neighboring country.

39

A Queen's Messenger

A few days after the Shell Kenya visit, John Bennett called to ask if I could do him a favor and entertain a colleague of his from London for dinner. He mentioned that the fellow was a queen's messenger from the diplomatic staff of the Foreign Office in London, and he personally brought highly confidential documents to and from several embassies. Of course, I was most interested to meet this fellow, as one never knew what could be learned from these encounters.

In the late afternoon, I went to the embassy and was introduced to Major K. D. Millar, queen's messenger. The gentleman was clearly a retired army officer, with a distinguished mustache and a very military bearing, straight-backed and rather formal. Having been a reserve army officer myself, I recognized the professional man behind the attitude, and I knew that what was seen on the outside was not necessarily what I could expect on the inside, particularly after a few drinks and some relaxed banter. Bennett put us on our way, and I took him to that now famous restaurant where I was a standard guest. We had a nice table with ample space around us to allow for a quiet discussion without having to fear that our conversation would be overheard. I ordered some cocktails, and I asked Major Millar to explain to me again the role of a queen's messenger. The Corps of Queen's Messengers, Major Millar explained, are couriers employed by the British Foreign and Commonwealth Office, who hand-carry secret and important documents to British embassies and consulates around the world. Many queen's messengers were retired army personnel such as he was. Messengers generally traveled in plain clothes in business class on scheduled airlines, carrying an official case from which they must not be separated; it may even be chained to their wrists.

He continued to tell me that the safe passage of diplomatic baggage is guaranteed by the Vienna Convention on Diplomatic Relations, and for reasons of state secrecy, the diplomatic bag does not go through normal airport baggage checks and must not be opened, x-rayed, weighed, or otherwise investigated by customs or airline security staff, or anyone else, for that matter. The bag is closed with a tamper-proof seal and has its own diplomatic passport.

The queen's messenger (QM) and his personal luggage, however, are not covered by special rules, so although the diplomatic bag, covered by the passport, is not checked, he and his personal luggage go through normal security screening. I was clearly expressing my fascination with this very special role within the diplomatic world, and, taken with my interest, Major Millar asked me if he could tell me the history behind the greyhound pattern on his tie. I had noted the tie and the design, but had not imagined that it had any special significance, so I asked him to tell me the story.

Major Millar said that the first recorded king's messenger was John Norman, who was appointed in 1485 by King Richard III, for whom he hand-delivered secret documents. While in exile, Charles II appointed four trusted men to convey messages to Royalist forces in England. As a sign of their authority, the king broke four silver greyhounds from a bowl familiar to royal courtiers and gave one to each man. A silver greyhound thus became the symbol of the service. On formal occasions, the queen's messengers wear this badge from a ribbon, and on less formal occasions, many messengers wear ties with a discreet greyhound pattern while working.[22]

Of course, he would not go into details about his current mission and diverted our conversation to my responsibilities and activities working for Shell in Burundi. I had plenty of stories to tell him, and we engaged in a lively conversation about the perils of life in African developing nations. The recent assassination of the prime minister was a topic of concern in the Foreign Office, as was the resulting expulsion of the Chinese. The whole situation in Central Africa had been changed with the denial of the Chinese attempt to secure a base of operations there. I told Millar that I was less concerned about the macro-problems, as the micro-problems were much more grassroots, such as delivery issues when the levels of the lakes were rising, and when LPG canisters were no longer available for home deliveries of gas for cooking purposes. I related to him at length my recent trip to Uganda and the reasons for the unexpected turn of

---

[22]   http://en.wikipedia.org/wiki/Queen's_Messenger.

events due to the Ugandan government's decision to close its border with Rwanda.

Millar seemed honestly interested in my stories, and we continued to talk through a good deal of the evening consuming not one, but a second bottle of excellent French wine. I dropped him off at his hotel, and he asked if he could again call upon me during a future visit, which he knew would be in a few weeks' time. I encouraged him to do so, and, indeed, nearly a month later, I did receive another call from John Bennett's office that Major Millar was in town again and would very much like to see me for dinner.

Once again we had a pleasant evening at the same restaurant. The discussion was lively, and as I had expected, Major Millar turned out to be less conservative than he had appeared during our very first encounter in the embassy. We chatted away, and we touched on the bachelor's life in such a remote place in Africa. The discussion turned to my previous engagement, during my time as a student in Lausanne, to Ann Wade, an American, which, as I explained to Major Millar, had ended due to some objections by my family.

I told him that I would like to meet Ann again during my next visit in England, but that I had not had a chance to arrange what would probably be a painful meeting. Major Millar suggested that he could be the right "messenger" in his official function. I laughed at his joke, but he was serious and agreed to contact Ann to send her my regards and suggest to her that we should meet for dinner next time I would be in London. I handed Ann's telephone number to Major Millar, and he promised to let me know the result of his effort to contact her.

Once again, we had a very nice evening, and we agreed to try to stay in touch. Indeed, a few weeks after his visit, I received a note in the mail from him that he had contacted Ann and met her for a drink. She was amenable to meet with me, and he suggested that I write to her to arrange for a date during my next visit in London. I was delighted to have this confirmation from the major, but I was not sure what the outcome of such a meeting would be. Major Millar and I never met again, but I have a fond memory of this special person in a very special profession, a queen's messenger, a real QM!

40

Paraffin Wax Sale to Collège du Saint-Esprit in Kitega

In between my meetings with Major Millar, business continued, and I made another trip to Kitega to visit my local clients. I would like to relate one visit, as it involved an infrequently sold product in Burundi, namely paraffin wax. Paraffin wax is used to make candles, and we had been selling this product in the past to the brothers at the Collège du Saint-Esprit, who fabricated candles to use in their church and for other purposes required by their religious ceremonies. I arrived at the Collège shortly before lunch, and our contact, one of the brothers, invited me to join them for a simple lunch. Indeed, it was simple, and I partook of their repast of French bread, a hot broth, and some grilled chicken, all the while discussing the situation in Burundi and the continued uncertainties in the Congo. They had been hearing horror stories about the persecution of members of various religious orders and the murders that had taken place during the uprising of the Simbas. I could not confirm any of these events, but I had also heard the same stories about the massacres.

Finally, we adjourned from the meal and our interesting discussions to proceed to the main purpose for my visit. Two brothers were charged with the purchases for the Collège, and they inquired about our pricing structure, as they had found that in the past they had been buying relatively small quantities of the paraffin wax, which seemed rather pricey for their production of a small quantity of candles.

I explained that if they would be willing to invest in the purchase of one metric ton of paraffin wax, it would be to their advantage, as the wax could be saved for a long time, since the product would not deteriorate, and I would give them a substantial discount on such a large purchase.

The brothers deliberated among themselves for a while and then asked about the cost of transportation. I told them that the cost of several small quantities to be shipped ex-Mombasa would be one of the reasons for the high retail charge, but to ship one metric ton would reduce the cost tremendously, including the wholesale price I would be able to offer them on a large order.

I left the two brothers with a signed order, and upon my return to the office, immediately processed it. I was not too surprised when I received a telex from our Shell office in Mombasa asking me to confirm my order for one metric ton of paraffin wax. The order was executed and paid by the Collège as per our order. I am sure that the brothers were happily making candles many a year after my departure from Burundi!

41

Communications in Burundi

Communications in Burundi were as difficult as I had experienced in Léopoldville, but were of vital importance to keep my superiors informed about the progress we were making and difficult business situations we encountered and had to resolve. It must have become clear that I was often left to my own devices when important decisions had to be made and that the results of such decisions were communicated to Léo after the fact.

To begin with, the mail service was barely functioning, resulting in a ten-day delay for regular mail to arrive in Léo from Bujumbura, so Paul Bröcker had clearly instructed me to only mail our monthly report and any nonessential documentation to the various managers. In addition, we had to make certain to have duplicates on file and not rely on the mail to be delivered, or to expect that mail would be delivered at all. Hence, all important mail we sent was confirmed as being mailed by telex, our other main means of communication. What would we have done without this marvel of technology? Our telex messages sent from

Bujumbura would arrive at best after two days at the Shell office in Léo, and, with some luck, I might have an answer two days later for a total turnaround time of four days. Since the responses would rarely be made the same day, we would have a five-day turnaround time, better than the two weeks we had, at best, with the mail.

During a coffee meeting with one of the managers of one of the other oil companies, I found that they had discovered a faster way to get their mail to their Léopoldville office. In short, they would put the mail in a large envelope and again put that envelope in a larger one and send the mail directly to their office in Brussels. They made sure that this envelope would leave on the plane from Bujumbura to Brussels, which departed daily in the late afternoon. The Brussels office had been instructed to take the second envelope from inside the larger one and mail this the day of arrival on the evening flight to Léo. This assured that the envelope would be in the office the next day or at worst the following day. This method cut the mailing time from ten days to two days, possibly three days.

I marveled at this opportunity and decided to try the same thing, but without prior consultation with my superiors. I sent a note with clear instructions with my double envelopes to the general manager of Belgium Shell and requested to know if they would be willing to support this improved way of communication from Shell Burundi to Shell Congo. I asked him to send me a telex to confirm that this would be acceptable and to let me know to whom I should be sending my envelopes in the future to ensure that this would get full attention and immediate execution.

The envelope was sent by Belgium Shell and forwarded to Shell in Léo. I received a telex from one of my colleagues in Brussels to direct any future mailings to him for future execution of this way of mailing my important messages. I thought that we would be adopting this procedure until I received a telex from my former boss, Henri van Zuylen, who admonished me in no uncertain terms that I had gone outside of the rule book regarding communicating with other Shell companies. He warned me not to repeat this way of mailing, as this was not approved by him, now the interim sales manager, and that I should not take such liberties in the future.

I was astounded to read this response, as I thought that improving our communications was vital to our operation and that the rule book could easily be adapted to the circumstances we were encountering. In any event, that closed the door on my borrowed scheme, and I advised my colleague in Brussels that henceforth, he would not be receiving any more envelopes for transit mailing to Léo.

Despite the dressing down I had received from Van Zuylen, upon my return to Léo a few months later, I found my correspondence in a file with notations by General Manager De Freitas that this was a great idea and should also be tried for our office in Goma! I never heard anything again about this issue, and Ivan de Stoop in Goma told me, upon my asking him, that he was never asked to initiate this scheme at his end. In the end, it confirmed to me that Henri was indeed too limited in his thinking and that his endless stay in Léo as an expat was probably just due to his lack of vision.

42

Letter from Carola Cutler

Frankly, I had forgotten about my father's intention to meet with Carola Cutler and her mother in New York City, so imagine my surprise when I received large envelope from the United States and, more specifically, from Carola!

She had been my girlfriend for a year, after her family moved to Wassenaar in the Netherlands from Paris in 1956, when I was all but sixteen years old. I had broken our relationship after returning from the USA, where I had been visiting family friends in North Carolina with a side visit to New York City. It had taken one month each way to cross the ocean from Europe to Hampton Roads in Virginia on a Norwegian freighter operating in charter for a Dutch shipping company, Vulkaan, at that time managed by my father. Upon my return after those two months, I was told by a friend that Carola had been dating an American student during my absence and hence my decision to break off our relationship. In any event, I went to the States again in 1960, after I had finished my two years of military service, traveling once again as a supernumerary on one of the chartered freighters of the Vulkaan. Carola, with whom I had still maintained a correspondence after she had returned to the United States in 1958, invited me to stay with her family.

Since my visit and stay at her home for ten days in 1960, I contacted her infrequently during the ensuing years. Frankly, had it not been for my father reestablishing the contact with her, I would not have thought too much about reconnecting. However, during my time in Bujumbura, I had been thinking about the bachelor's life as a member of the Shell family. My conclusion was rather uncertain on that score. Although I felt that I would not gladly go to my next posting for the company without a partner, I played with the idea that I should consider potential candidates for marital life. I mused about the idea of using my two months' home leave to meet again with some of the ladies I had in mind. It had not occurred to me that this approach toward marriage might not necessarily be the smartest way!

I opened the package and began reading the letter, in which Carola described at length her current activities since she had graduated from the University of Connecticut. She was working in New York City at WOR, a radio station owned by General Tire, the employer of her father, who had moved to Morocco to be head of the Middle East, and general manager for General Tire in Morocco. Her mother had remarried her father and was now living part of the year in Darien, Connecticut, specifically to make a home for Carola and her brother, Fred, who was still in high school.

Well, I was fully brought up to date through the letter, but what piqued my interest was the colored photograph she had included of herself that showed a beautiful young woman, now all of twenty-four. My juices started flowing, and I decided that I would accept her invitation, but first I replied to her letter without alluding to my potential visit and waited for a reply, which ultimately reached me upon my return to Léopoldville, a month or so later. However, my mind was starting to set upon my marriage idea, and it would occupy me until my departure from Léo.

43

Birthday Celebrations
for Mwami Mwambutsa IV

Mwami Mwambutsa IV on his throne

**Burundi Royal Drummers and Dancers
performing for the Mwami**

Burundi Royal Drummers and Dancers

Katharina, my secretary, came into my office with an official-looking envelope and exclaimed: "Mr. Van den Houten, guess what, you have been invited to the birthday party for the mwami in Kitega!" I had no idea that the mwami's birthday was imminent, nor did I know what this meant until I received a call from John Bennett's secretary, who asked me if she could have a ride to the mwami's birthday event. I asked her whether she could not go with her boss, Ambassador Bennett, but she said that he had a ride with a few other members of the diplomatic corps and would not be in the same area as those invited from the business community. I asked her what this would be all about, and she explained that the mwami's birthday was an opportunity to see the famous Royal Drummers of Burundi.

Although Paul had told me about the annual sorghum celebration, he had not mentioned the mwami's birthday. I was already very curious about the event, so it did not matter if it was a birthday, or other celebration. The ceremonial aspect was the real thing to witness! Of course, I invited Bennett's secretary to ride with me to the event.

I told our Burundi sales representative, a Tutsi, that I was going to the birthday celebration of the mwami, whereupon he explained the history and customs surrounding this event. It would be held in the hills close to Kitega, an area known as the Higiro Hill, a sacred area where the Royal *Inakigabiro* (lady of the land) drums were kept.

A very important drum is the *rukinzo*; it accompanied the mwami everywhere he went, although I never saw this drum in the nightclub, when I encountered the mwami some months earlier. He continued to tell me that the drums were used for special occasions such as the mwami's birthday and the already-mentioned festival of the sowing of the sorghum, named *omuganuru*. However, my colleague added that some of the ancient rituals were not strictly adhered to, but that the drums were still brought out for special occasions and maintained a special place in the veneration of the mwami. Hence, the absence of the drum in the nightclub!

We drove to Kitega on the main route and finally started to drive up the hill to the Higiro Hill. Traffic was increasing, and a tremendous number of people were walking toward the location where the event was taking place. After parking the car, we were shown the way to the special area for invited guests and were soon enjoying a beer and a sandwich.

The crowds were growing, and we were told to go outside to the enclosures, as the drummers would be arriving at any time to start their performances. We walked toward an open terrain where the drummers were expected. While we were waiting for the action to start, we were joined by a longtime Belgian resident of Bujumbura known to both of us who started telling us about more of the action we would be witnessing. "The performance of the Royal Drummers has been the same for centuries, and their techniques and traditions are passed down from father to son. The members of the ensemble take turns playing the central drum, the *Inkiranya*, dancing, resting, and playing the other drums, rotating throughout the show without interruptions," he explained. At the start of their performance, the drummers enter balancing the heavy drums on their heads and singing and playing. In addition to the *Inkiranya*, there are *Amashako* drums that provide a continuous beat, and the *Ibishikiso* drums that follow the rhythm established by the

Inkiranya.[23] Some extra members carry ornamental spears and shields and lead the procession with their dance. They then perform a series of rhythms; some accompanied by song, and exit the stage the same way, carrying the drums on their heads while playing.

Burundi Royal Drummers and Dancers

---

[23] www.burundidrummers.com/about-us; http://music.africa museum.be/instruments/english/burundi/burundi.html.

More Royal Drummers and Dancers

Just as our Belgian friend finished telling us about the history of the Royal Drummers, the first dancers arrived. The tall and slender Tutsis were dressed in leopard skins and wrapped with strings of beads and brandished long spears. Jumping up and down to the rhythms of the drums, which indeed were carried on the heads of the drummers, they led the way for the procession of some forty drummers, who lined up in two rows leaving ample room for the dancers to continue their dances in between. The one row of drums, made of hollowed-out tree trunks covered with animal skins held down with wooden pegs, was beaten in a steady, continuous beat. The other row of drums was following the rhythms established by one central drum, the *Inkiranya*. We were absolutely fascinated by the performance, which continued unabated for nearly an hour.

Just as described by my Tutsi representative, the mwami was still sitting on his throne with a continuous stream of his subjects emerging from the hills in the distance, walking to him with their loads of gifts on their heads and towing a variety of cattle to the open field in front of the mwami. The Belgian told us that these presentations and the dancing would continue until the mwami had enough of sitting on his throne and then would descend to the diplomatic enclosure to greet the guests there.

We returned to the businessmen's enclosure and enjoyed more of the food and libations. I was astounded to see some of the guests throwing food and bottles of beer across the hedges separating us from the regular folks, who were pressing in ever-greater numbers against the hedges to try to get some of the food and especially bottles of beer tossed to them by the guests.

My companion and I stayed for another hour, conversing with other members of the business community, notably the other oil company executives, as well as a few of my clients. It was a spectacular gathering, and the aura of the mwami and his drummers was felt by all of us.

We returned to Bujumbura reveling in the traditional dancing and particularly the remarkable performance of the drummers. It certainly was something that would remain in my memory as one of the highlights of the Burundi culture that I witnessed during my stay in the country.

44

Final Month in Bujumbura and Return of Paul and Monique Bröcker

The total sales results in Rwanda, together with the LPG revenues during the various crises, resulted in a very positive reaction from my superiors in Léo, and I was asked to send a few explanatory telexes about the political situation to both the sales manager and the general manager. The positive results did not lie, and I took full pride in my handling of the unforeseen situation in Rwanda. The sales book, handed to me by Paul, included a graph that showed such a spike that it needed a foldout, as the sales figures exceeded the size of the page in the book! But now, as Paul and Monique's return to Bujumbura approached, I settled into more of a routine, still with curfew and still making my nightly trips after curfew wearing my black beret and safari suit. They returned in the second week of March after a home leave of three months. I met them at the airport, and Paul immediately started to bombard me with questions. He had not been aware of all the developments in the country, which had not been reported in the areas they had been visiting during their home leave, such as the news of the assassination of Prime Minister Pierre Ngendandumwe and the subsequent troubles with the Chinese, nor the rising of the waters of the lake and the disturbances with the border closure between Uganda and Rwanda.

We returned to the bungalow, and Monique immediately invited me to stay with them, although I had arranged to stay in a downtown hotel. Monique would not have it, and I canceled the hotel, unpacked my suitcases, and reinstalled myself in the room I had gladly occupied during their absence.

We stayed at home that evening, as I had already arranged for the cook to prepare a welcome home dinner. Paul's favorite Primus beer had been stocked in the fridge, and while he partook of his brew, Monique and I enjoyed a whiskey with water. Paul could not wait to hear my account of the events of the last three months. I elaborated about all that had happened, and by the time we rolled into bed, well warmed by the alcoholic beverages, I thought he was not too displeased that he had been away during this time. Yet, he seemed concerned about the status of the books in the office, as he kept asking if everything had been kept in good order. I kept reassuring him that, thanks to the assistance of our secretary and representatives for both countries, he would not find any discrepancies in the recorded results.

The next day, we went to the office, and after his rounds of greetings with the employees, we settled in to start the process of the hand-back of responsibilities. The first thing that Paul was interested in was his sales book with the odd foldout page demonstrating the peak in the sales of our gasoline in Rwanda. He could not believe that we had sold such an amount, and I had to explain again what had happened during the border closure, as well as the events preceding the closure. Paul seemed very concerned about the unauthorized trip Ivan de Stoop and I had taken to Uganda.

I showed him the telex I received from De Freitas, commending me on the initiative, as well as on the resulting sales results. Yet, Paul demonstrated to me once again that he was not the entrepreneurial type and, like Henri van Zuylen in Léo, was more prone to strictly following the book. This was a bit contrary to his earlier decision to charter a plane in Léo to fly back to Bujumbura, but I noted that he had acted in that case more out of fear than out of a rationally considered decision. During the next few weeks, we spent time visiting several of our clients to bid my farewell and to assure them that Shell was back in Paul's good hands.

I had a very nice farewell lunch with Ambassador Bennett and a few of the acquaintances I had made in the last few months. Paul also arranged for a final luncheon with the office staff. The staff had arranged for a gift to me in commemoration of my stay in Bujumbura. I truly appreciated their gesture, and I took pains to thank all of them for the way they had supported me during my time as their manager. I especially took time to thank Katharina Loval, who during my time in Burundi had been a very loyal and trusted secretary. She deserved my thanks for all her extra attention to issues of the management of the office during my frequent absences traveling on company business. I would miss her professional attitude and her cheerful presence.

Paul booked my flight for March 20 to return to Léopoldville. With only a few more days left, I spent my time cleaning up a few outstanding matters concerning our sales reports and documents that had to go to the Ministry of Finance pertaining to the period I had been responsible for Shell's operations. I also had a brief telex exchange with Ivan de Stoop, thanking him for his support and friendship during my stay and particularly his contribution to our successful effort to keep Rwanda supplied during the recent border closing. This would be my last and final contact with Ivan. The same would be true of my contact with Paul Bröcker and his charming wife Monique; they continued to stay in Burundi, at least during the remaining time I spent in the Congo.

45

Return to Léopoldville—Assistant Manager Aviation Products

The flight to Léo was uneventful. I spent my time reflecting on the past five months, as well as wondering what my next responsibility would be for the remaining weeks of my assignment. I had not been told by management what they had in store for me, but it did not worry me too much, as I felt that I had done a reasonably good job out in the sticks of Bujumbura and Rwanda. We had survived a great number of crises, and I had increased the sales in both countries considerably, despite the political turmoil.

I sat back and thought about the fact that in just over a month, I would be leaving for a two months' home leave. It would be great to see my parents and sisters again in Brussels and visit with friends in the Netherlands. I knew from my Shell colleagues that all expats had to report to London for a debriefing regarding the last assignment and to discuss the next career steps Shell had in store. It all would be exciting, and not knowing at this stage made the mystery of one's future quite thrilling.

I also started to think about my meeting with Ann Wade again in London, and the thought started to solidify that I might travel to the United States to meet with Carola in New York and Connecticut. I also thought about meeting another old flame, Ann Dickinson, who had returned to the Boston area after a great number of years in my hometown of Wassenaar, where we had been "pinned" for at least a year at one point. All these interesting and appealing thoughts were drifting through my mind.

I was met at the airport by a Shell car, and as they had indicated to me by telex, I was taken to the Shell office/apartment building, where I was shown the smallish bachelor apartment, where I would be spending my final days in Léopoldville. I found my personal belongings all stacked in boxes in the apartment, and that evening Leslie Armstrong, our human resources manager, and his wife invited me to dinner in their apartment in the Shell building. Leslie was well-informed about the events that transpired in Bujumbura, and he complimented me on the way I had conducted myself during the assignment.

During our meal, I learned that in addition to the Bak family, who had left before my departure for Burundi, Jim and Margaret Don and their kids had also left, as Jim had been assigned to Algeria as the chief accountant. His replacement as treasurer, Jean-Claude Moutet, a Frenchman, had arrived, and I would meet him the next day. Rudolf Bak had been replaced by an English bachelor, Jeremy Farrington, who had arrived a few months earlier. He was scheduled to have lunch with me, together with Jean-Claude Moutet, to bring me up to speed with the events in Léo during my absence.

I was quite tired after the flight and withdrew early, collapsing in bed, wondering once more what would be next. Leslie had not divulged my next job, which he said would be left to the country sales manager, Becker, who would fill me in the next morning and further debrief me.

The next morning, I met with Becker, who was a lot more cordial to me than he had been in the past. Clearly, my performance in Burundi was well-received by him, and he mentioned briefly that I had lived up to my promise in my letter to him and had erased the negative impressions he had formed about me during my first months of my assignment in Léo. He mentioned that I was assigned for my next job to the position of assistant manager of the Aviation Department.

I would be reporting directly to the Aviation Department's manager, a Frenchman by the name of Jean Olivier. He immediately took me with him to meet with Olivier, who welcomed me cordially and invited me to join him and his wife that evening for dinner. It appeared I had been reintegrated into the social whirl of Léo quite fast.

Jean-Claude Moutet and Jeremy Farrington met me for lunch the same day, and we had a very nice meal together. We seemed to click immediately, and I invited both to join me that coming weekend on the river. Jean-Claude was now living in the same house where Jim and Margaret Don had been living, opposite my former home in Parque Hembise. He invited me for dinner the next evening so I could meet his wife, Monique. I also quickly called John Rutherford, the banker to whom I had entrusted my boat, and told him I would like to go on the river the coming weekend with two new Shell colleagues. John thanked me for the use of the boat and asked if I would be interested in selling it to him at the end of my tour. I told him immediately that we would have a deal if I could still use the boat during the remainder of my stay. He agreed to my price of $1,500, and said he had no problem with my use of the boat for the next month or so.

The next few weeks went by with a few more social encounters. Loukina van der Werf, De Freitas's secretary, had been transferred and was replaced by a tiny English girl, Melanie Carter, who was in her early twenties. Melanie lived in an apartment across from the Shell Building, and she invited me for dinner as soon as we met.

My attempt to pick up again with Gilberte, the Swiss gal with whom I had a torrid affair prior to my departure for Bujumbura, did not work out too well, as she apparently had found another lover and was no longer available. My attempts to see her, or at least to meet her again for dinner, were rebuked, and I decided not to waste any additional time and acknowledged that our past episode was history.

Melanie offered another romantic opportunity I had not expected, as our dinner in her apartment rapidly turned into an affair, which lasted exactly that one evening! It was a bit awkward afterward, as we ran into each other daily, but the alcohol-induced one-night stand left no ill feelings, and we remained very cordial to each other for the remainder of my stay.

Dinner at the Moutets was a delightful start of a new friendship, and while we knew that I would be leaving in just about a month, we felt like we had known each other for years. Jean Claude had been educated in part in the United States and spoke excellent American-accented English, no small feat for a Frenchman, and he acknowledged that languages were not necessarily a strength of the French. Monique was also a very warm and charming hostess, and we spent a delightful evening talking about their first impressions of Léo, and I told them a great number of stories relating to my five months in Burundi and Rwanda. We knew that we had found a common ground for a friendship that we all wished would last beyond our time spent in the Congo.

The next weekend, we took my boat to the islands, and I met a great number of my former acquaintances on one of our familiar sandbanks. Still I found the absence of the Bak and Don families a bit sad, and it brought to me the understanding that the Shell expat life was one of short, intense friendships, especially in this country with all the additional pressures brought about due to the uncertain and often dangerous political circumstances.

46

My Next Assignment

During the next few weeks, I was getting back into a routine of dealing with orders in the Aviation Department and calling on a few of the airlines that were our customers. The assignment did not carry any major responsibilities, and after a week it became clear to me that this was a mere parking station for me until my departure.

I just kept my new boss, Jean Olivier, closely informed, and he, in turn, made sure to involve me with the broader activities of our department. Basically, my day started and ended without any glamour or the excitement I had experienced in Bujumbura. Of course, we were all kept informed about the progress of the political developments in the east of the country. Stanleyville, now liberated, apparently was still a complete mess, as was much of the area where the Simbas had raised havoc among the population on their warpath. The subsequent activities of the government troops, led by the mercenaries of the renowned Colonel Hoar, were even more devastating to the region. But we didn't hear about the true developments, as the local paper gave us no information of any substance, nor did the international press reach us on time. So, we continued to rely on the information from our diplomatic acquaintances and the office grapevine.

Finally, I received a call from Melanie that De Freitas would like to see me right away in his office. I knew that this would be the important announcement of my next posting with Shell, so I hurried down the stairs to meet him. Melanie showed me into his office at once, and George waved me into a chair. "Hans, your efforts have been recognized, and we are pleased to let you know that your next assignment will be in South Africa."

I immediately expressed my excitement about this most interesting country, but De Freitas interrupted me, wondering if I might not first like to know about my new position with Shell South Africa? He proceeded to tell me that I was assigned to the operations manager of the Transvaal in the Regional Head Office in Johannesburg as his personal assistant, or PA. I would be involved in special projects at the direction of the OM, and I would start the job immediately after my two-month home leave, which would begin in less than two weeks.

I expressed my thanks to De Freitas for the news and wondered how long I would be posted in South Africa. De Freitas responded that it would be for at least two years, but that he had no idea of the exact duration. During my visit in London, where I was expected to meet with the regional staff, I would receive more extensive instructions, as well as more feedback about my career development. De Freitas urged me to get all my affairs arranged and to let him know the date of my departure. I returned to my office jubilantly and started to make a few calls to my colleagues to tell them the exciting news of my new posting to South Africa.

Before the end of the day, the customary farewell party routine was also set in motion with many invitations for luncheons and dinners coming my way. Jean-Claude and Monique immediately offered to give me a farewell party at their home and it continued, with colleagues and friends offering their congratulations on this fine new assignment.

Leslie Armstrong, still our personnel manager, sprang into action and immediately fixed my departure date for April 23 for Brussels. A few days later, he also confirmed my flight to London and my visitation schedule at the head office of Shell. I would spend just two days with my parents in Brussels and then onward to London. Despite the whirlwind of parties in anticipation of my departure from the Congo, I did have time to reflect on the past year, and more so about my future, specifically the next two months of home leave.

Of course, my visit to Brussels was to be a family reunion of a few days before I would be off to London, where I had arranged to meet many friends. But above all, I was to meet my former fiancée, Ann Wade. I had been reflecting on this get-together after our breakup, and I could not imagine how this would develop. In any event, I had no specific feelings left other than a degree of remorse over the way we had separated at the beginning of the previous year, before I had left for the Congo. I also felt very strongly that I wished to explore a more permanent relationship, and not necessarily with Ann.

Consequently, I arranged to fly from London to New York to meet with Carola, where I was scheduled to stay a week or so, prior to departing for Boston, where I did manage to arrange to meet that lovely former flame, Ann Dickinson. She had returned to the United States with her family after spending a great number of years in Wassenaar, a suburb of The Hague in the Netherlands, where her father headed a major American insurance company in Europe. In any event, I had no other plans than to see if any amorous liaisons would redevelop, be it New York or Boston. Otherwise, I felt that my year in the Congo had been a very educational and exciting experience. I certainly had grown in my personal capabilities as a businessman.

The stressful months in Burundi and the way I had managed Shell's business in a profitable way, despite the distressing circumstances, was something that made me feel proud of my achievements. I felt ready for a broader challenge and a higher level of responsibility, which South Africa might well offer me in my next career move.

47

Sale of Volkswagen and Packing Up

In addition to the party routine, which was dominating my evenings, I arranged for the moving company to pack my belongings. The Personnel Department would handle the ultimate details of shipping my stuff to Johannesburg. In addition to making sure my itinerary was properly completed, I rushed off a few letters to my parents, as well as to Ann Wade, Carola Cutler, and Ann Dickinson to confirm my arrival.

One important issue I had to deal with was the sale of my Volkswagen. Once again Luc Vossen, who had arranged upon my arrival for my driver's license, put out the word into his network of local Shell clients that my VW was available for sale. Only a few days later, he introduced me to a Congolese, who arrived at the office very formally dressed in suit and tie, carrying a black briefcase and requesting to see my VW. He asked me to confirm the sales price, which I had put at $1,500, just about what I had paid for the car in equivalent guilders the previous year in the Netherlands.

Since I had paid back the loan to Shell during the past year, I would have a nice amount saved. Upon seeing the car, which had been serviced and washed, the Congolese seemed very pleased, and, returning to my office, he agreed to buy the car on the spot. The black briefcase was put on the table, and he opened it to reveal bundles of Congolese francs. Counting the equivalent amount converted at the black-market rate of 6.50 francs to the dollar, he handed me a large bundle and asked for the keys, and I escorted him to the VW. He started the car, and off he went, leaving me standing without transportation! I was in luck, though, as Leslie Armstrong arranged for a car to be at my disposal for my final days in Léo. However, now I was left with a bundle of Congolese francs, and I had to dispose of them quickly to get my dollars or Belgian francs into my account in Brussels. Thus, that very afternoon and evening, I put all the cash into two shoe sleeves and started to make the tour of my friends and colleagues. A few I could find in their offices, but most of my evening was spent sipping cocktails and exchanging the Congolese francs against the black-market rate for checks in dollars or Belgian francs, drawn on European banks. That was the way it had been for the last year, a trust all of us had with each other that the checks would clear and not bounce. I had no bad experiences with any of them, and I happily exchanged the Congolese francs for a small bundle of checks that I would deposit into my bank account upon my arrival in Brussels.

48

Last Meeting with George de Freitas

My final days were upon me, as I enjoyed the round of luncheons, cocktails, and dinners so customary in Léo for those arriving and leaving the country. I made a lot of good friends, including those during my last few weeks since I had returned from Bujumbura. Jean-Claude and Monique had become real pals; they had been very hospitable to a lone bachelor, and many a night we were together not only at the parties, but often afterward to enjoy nightcaps. Jeremy Farrington, also a bachelor, often joined us in these escapades. In addition, a great number of the former group with whom I had enjoyed the weekends on the river was invited. Life seemed good and the future bright.

George de Freitas invited me for drinks at his house a few days before my departure. Upon my arrival, his "boy" brought me into the library, which included a bar, and gave me a whiskey. Then George entered wrapped in a towel and apologizing that he was not properly dressed, as he had just finished a swim in his pool. I was delighted that he took this informal approach with one of his junior staff.

George, with whom I had not spent a minute alone except for the two occasions in his office when I heard about my assignments in Burundi and South Africa, started to ask me about my personal background, and soon we were talking about my experiences in the Congo. He expressed his thanks again for a job well done. He added that he felt that I had done remarkably well, by not only increasing our sales, but also in creating a very positive image of the company. He revealed that he had heard positive comments about me from the British Embassy. I suspected that Ambassador Bennett had been passing information to George regarding my performance, which did not surprise me, as Bennett and I had truly worked quite closely together, and he had been observing me during my stay and witnessed firsthand my various exploits. George also revealed that he had been talking to his counterpart in Kenya, who had visited Bujumbura and whose office had been closely involved with me during the flooding of the railway in Kenya, as well as the supply delays during the rising of Lake Tanganyika.

There we sat together for a few hours, George in his towel wrap and I formally dressed in shirt and tie, but I enjoyed being able to talk at liberty to this very interesting and distinguished gentleman. George finally said good-bye, but not before telling me that his driver would take me to the airport. I felt honored by this gesture. At the end of our get-together, we shook hands, and I asked him to make sure to look me up if ever he would visit South Africa during my stay. I left his home feeling great to have had such a nice and personal few hours with the boss, and his gestures toward me and my performance gave me a further feeling of satisfaction of a job well done.

49

Departure from the Congo

Finally, April 23 arrived, and my departure was set three weeks short of my arrival the previous year! The apartment was looking drab without any of my personal belongings, but I was happy to be on my way. Suitcase packed and delivered to the car by De Freitas's driver, I started to make my final rounds of good-byes to my colleagues. I was glad I had taken extra time to do so, because with few exceptions we engaged in lengthy recollections of the past year. I had no idea if I would ever see some of them again, especially those who were not international expats.

It turned out to be a warm tour through the offices, and finally I stepped into George de Freitas's office for a last farewell and a handshake. He accompanied me to his car and instructed his driver to make sure I would be leaving the country safely. I sat myself on the plush backseat of his limousine, and with a final wave to George, the car pulled away, and with a last look over my shoulder, I bade farewell to the Shell building. Without a hitch, we arrived at the airport, and the driver helped me through the formalities, which surprisingly took little time and effort and not a single demand came my way for a *matabisch*, or bribe, to either have my passport returned or my bag properly tagged and dispatched to the plane. I said farewell to the Shell driver and entered the lounge, waiting to be called to board.

We walked to the bottom of the stairs, and in the now familiar humidity and heat, we started boarding the plane. At the top of the stairs, I turned around and had another look at the airport buildings, which were not especially attractive, nor was the airport, but it was a look that was a final one, for my days in the Congo had come to an end.

I took my seat at a window, and soon the Sabena airline hostess closed the door. I thought about my arrival a year earlier at the airport of Kano, when the door had opened and the "envelope" of my African stay had invited me into its enclosure. Now with the closure of the door, the envelope sealed, and experiences—some bad, but mostly good—were contained and locked into my memories of one year in Africa.

Acknowledgments

It has taken many years to put my recollections to paper, and during this time, I was encouraged by a great number of my former colleagues and friends, to whom I occasionally sent a completed chapter. I owe my thanks to Marlies and Rudolf Bak for the additional input to put our recollections in focus from my early days in Léopoldville. To this day, I am grateful for the care provided to me by Marlies when I suffered my first bout with dysentery, and our enduring friendship is very special and treasured. We see each other regularly in the Netherlands, where we live not far from each other, which is a treat.

My thanks also go out to Jim and Margaret Don, living in Annapolis, Maryland, USA, with whom I still have a lot of contact. When they visited Almelo, where I now reside with my wife, Marian, I had the pleasure to talk with them again about our days in Léo. I owe my thanks to Marian for her support and encouragement, but above all, her patience with my absences behind the computer that got my story into shape. This last element of a book is obviously a very important aspect of the writer's work.

One never sees all the grammatical and spelling mistakes, as well as the correct punctuations, so the eye and knowledge of the editor is of utmost importance to get the final version prepared and acceptable for publication. Therefore, I cannot be more grateful to Julie Kennedy Cochran for her voluntary support and editing of my manuscript.

Julie and I spent a lot of hours sending chapters back and forth to each other, and she made a great number of very helpful suggestions to the context of this story. I benefited from her careful reading of my work, in addition to all the editorial suggestions, to make the outcome understandable and clear to the reader. Julie, my thanks and a big hug for all your friendship and a great editing job. You allowed my style and approach to the context of this story, *One Year in Africa*, to stay as it was; yet, you improved the manuscript to a happy ending.

At the suggestion of my son, Andrew, I connected with Dianna Downing, who had another look at the near final draft of my memoir. Her expert editing of the grammar, spelling, and structuring of the prose used was a final and great enhancement of the linguistic quality of the story. I thank Dianna for her assistance, and Andrew for having made the connection.

My publisher, AuthorHouse, provided me also with an excellent final review of my memoir. Their editors were most helpful to ensure that my text was correct with grammar, punctuation, spelling, and syntax, in line with AuthorHouse's house style, which is based largely on the style prescriptions of *The Chicago Manual of Style*.

Finally, I would like to add that the experience with Royal Dutch Shell in Africa was very valuable for my career development, and, frankly, if I had not decided to follow a different path in life, I would have stayed my entire career with this exceptional company, as I felt comfortable with the oil flowing through my veins!

About the Author

Hans van den Houten was born in the Netherlands on August 6, 1940. After his economic studies at the University of Lausanne, he graduated in 1963 as a *Licence ès Science Economique et Sociale*, which is accepted in the Netherlands as a *Doctorandus Economie*, or Drs. for short.

Following the period described in this memoir, he moved to South Africa and married Carola Cutler, a US citizen, and left Shell in 1967 to immigrate to the United States with Carola. They had three children, Tania, their daughter, born in 1970; Saskia, another daughter, born in 1977, who died at the age of three months due to a congenital heart problem; and Andrew, their son, born in 1979.

He joined the Chase Manhattan Bank in 1967 and completed the credit training program in 1969. Prior to his appointment as assistant treasurer of the bank, he became involved with a special project for the Museum of Modern Art. Because of his recommendations, he was asked by the Executive Board of MOMA to join the museum for a period of three years in 1970. Granted a leave of absence by Chase, he restructured the museum's financial administration as the director of finance and chief financial officer.

Hans returned to Chase in 1973 as a vice president and had several assignments in the Far East, as well as French-speaking Africa. He left Chase in 1976 and continued his career as vice president of Moody's Investors Service, a credit rating agency in New York City, where he restarted its international division. After three years, he was promoted to Dun & Bradstreet International, a sister company of Moody's in the D&B Corporation, where he became the vice president and regional manager for Latin America. In 1984, he left D&B and joined Fitch Investor Service, where he started the international operations of Fitch, another leading rating agency, and moved to London to implement his recommendation to start EuroRatings, a European-based rating agency for Fitch and other investors.

Returning to the United States in 1988 from London, he joined the boutique executive recruiting firm of E. J. Lance Management. In 1991, he was recruited to Republic National Bank, where until 1999 he was first vice president, responsible for all of Republic's international corporate banking activities. After the sale of Republic to HSBC, he rejoined E. J. Lance and spent another three years in the executive recruiting world, until he was recruited himself to head the Senior Management Executive Counseling Department of Lee Hecht Harrison, as senior vice president in New York in 2004.

On April 30, 2003, he was awarded, by Queen Beatrix of the Netherlands, a knighthood in the Order of Orange-Nassau (Ridder in de Orde van Oranje-Nassau) for his multiple contributions to the strengthening of the relations between the Netherlands and the United States of America.

Following his divorce from Carola in 1987, who passed away, following a three-year fight with cancer, on December 30, 2015, he married in 1987 with Rebecca Boone Alston, a Mississippi native, and an architect and artist. They separated in 2004.

On July 8, 2005, Hans married Marian Scholten-Was, widow of his Lausanne former fellow student Tony Scholten. Following their marriage, Hans retired in October 2005, and they are now splitting their time between their homes in Bend, Oregon, and Almelo, the Netherlands.

)

CPSIA information can be obtained
at www.ICGtesting.com
Printed in the USA
FSOW03n2129200317
32143FS